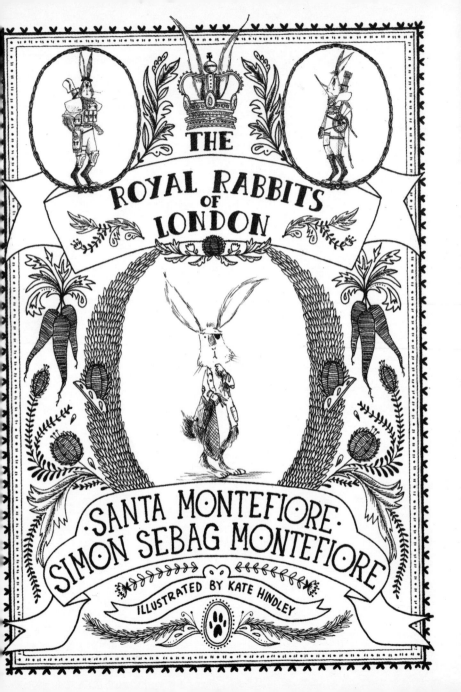

THE
ROYAL RABBITS
OF
LONDON

·SANTA MONTEFIORE·
SIMON SEBAG MONTEFIORE

ILLUSTRATED BY KATE HINDLEY

First published in Great Britain in 2016 by Simon and Schuster UK Ltd
A CBS COMPANY

Text Copyright © Simon Sebag Montefiore and Santa Montefiore 2016
Illustrations Copyright © Kate Hindley 2016

7 9 10 8

Simon & Schuster UK Ltd
1st Floor, 222 Gray's Inn Road
London
WC1X 8HB

www.simonandschuster.co.uk
www.simonandschuster.com.au
www.simonandschuster.co.in

Simon & Schuster Australia, Sydney
Simon & Schuster India, New Delhi

A CIP catalogue record for this book is available from the British Library.

PB ISBN 978-1-4711-5788-2
eBook ISBN 978-1-4711-5787-5

Printed and bound by CPI Group (UK) Ltd, Croydon, CR0 4YY

Simon & Schuster UK Ltd are committed to sourcing paper that is made from
wood grown in sustainable forests and supports the Forest Stewardship Council,
the leading international forest certification organisation. Our books displaying
the FSC logo are printed on FSC certified paper.

To our darling son, Sasha,
who conceived this book

THE WEEPING WILLOW AT GREEN PARK

THE RIVER THAMES.

BUCKINGHAM PALACE

ROYAL RABBIT H.Q

THE RABBIT KINGDOM

buck male rabbit

bunkin country rabbit

bunny young rabbit

doe female rabbit

Hopster large, strong and clever rabbit

Thumper Special Forces
commando rabbit

CHAPTER ONE

In a deep, dark burrow at the edge of the forest, Horatio, the old grey rabbit, heard the rustle of leaves and the patter of paws. He put down his book, ears sharp, and sat up straight in the big, tatty armchair where he had been warming himself in front of the fire.

Horatio was elderly and grizzled, and a stump was all that remained of his hind left paw, but his hearing was as good as ever and he listened carefully as the footsteps grew louder. The old rabbit's heartbeat quickened and he began to slide the handle from his walking stick, easing a blade into the

dim light.

When a rabbit has been hunted by his enemies who want to kill him, he never sleeps easy again. 'Who twitches there?' he demanded, looking over the cracked frame of his spectacles. His voice sounded strangely gruff, more like a dog's growl than a rabbit's murr.

'It's me, Shylo Tawny-Tail,' replied a soft voice nervously. In the doorway, Shylo gave a gentle thump of his hind paw — for that is what polite rabbits do when they arrive somewhere — and twitched his nose.

Horatio relaxed and slid the sword back into his walking stick. 'Come in, young Shylo Tawny-Tail,' he said. But the small, skinny rabbit hesitated for, although he had visited Horatio more than a dozen times now, the old buck was still an alarming sight.

'Don't be afraid! You've come back for more stories about the Old World, have you?' murred Horatio, whose smile revealed a broken yellow tooth.

'Yes,' Shylo replied, lolloping into the gloomy room.

Horatio looked at Shylo's narrow shoulders, his scrawny body, the red eyepatch worn to correct his squint and he had yet to see a weaker and more feeble bunny. But Horatio knew that looks could be deceiving. After all, hadn't he been just as weak and feeble once? Hadn't he then risen to great heights?

He smiled at the courage of the small bunny because not only was it forbidden by the Leaders of the Warren to venture this close to the farm, but it was also absolutely and totally and unmistakably forbidden to visit Horatio.

When Horatio had arrived here all those years ago, broken in both body and mind, not to mention strange in manner, for he belonged to a very different variety of rabbit, they had barred their burrows against him. He had been forced to build a home on the other side of the forest, only a short distance from the farm that nestled in the valley below.

Indeed, fear of strangers was a terrible thing. But Shylo's curiosity seemed so much greater than his initial fear. Indeed,

it was his curiosity that had led the little bunny to Horatio's burrow in the first place and was what kept him coming back again and again.

'So where does your mother think you are this time?' Horatio asked.

'I said I was going to dig up turnips,' Shylo replied, one ear flopping over his forehead in embarrassment because, as lies go, it wasn't a very good one.

'Well, no one will find you in this part of the forest, that's for sure.'

Horatio pointed at the store cupboard with a shaky paw that was always wrapped in a bandage. 'You'll find a bag of turnips in there. I can't send you back empty-handed. You know you could get into a lot of trouble coming to see me.'

'Mother says you're . . .' Shylo hesitated suddenly because what his mother said about Horatio wasn't very polite.

'Mad?' Horatio finished the sentence with a chuckle, then erupted into a fit of coughing. 'I know what they say. That

I've lost my mind and that my enemies will find me here and put everyone in terrible danger. Fear is born out of ignorance, Shylo Tawny-Tail. Don't ever forget that. Your Leaders don't know any better.'

Shylo gazed at the long scar on the old buck's cheek, the bandaged paw, the ugly stump of his missing fourth paw and his left ear which seemed to have been almost entirely bitten off, and he understood why other rabbits were afraid of crazy Horatio. The old rabbit looked like he'd had a fight with Tobias the farm cat, and won. But Shylo had discovered, quite by chance, that the battle-scarred buck was really a surprisingly gentle rabbit once you got to know him.

Horatio took off his glasses. 'Sit down, Shylo. Now where did we finish last time?'

Shylo went to the bookcase and pulled down a large, heavy book and carried it, rather unsteadily, across the room. He perched on the stool beside Horatio and pushed the book, covered in cobwebs, on to the big buck's knee. Horatio read

out its title: '*The Rise and Fall of the Great Rabbit Empire.*'

'You were telling me about the Great Rabbit Empire,' murred Shylo eagerly. 'When the Great Rabbits of England governed much of the Rabbit World. At that time, most of the Human World was ruled by the Great British Empire. As above, so below, I believe you said. Then both empires fell–'

'Yes, the British lost many of the lands they'd conquered in faraway places and so did the Great Rabbits,' Horatio interrupted. 'Now America is the most powerful country in the *Human* World and the American rabbits are the most powerful in the *Rabbit* World. But let's go back to the beginning. Tell me about the oath made long ago to protect the Royal Family. Tell me about that band of elite rabbits.'

Shylo's eyes shone with excitement. 'Many hundreds of years ago, when King Arthur ruled England, he declared that rabbit pie should be the favourite meal of the kingdom. But his seven-year-old nephew, Prince Mordred, loved rabbits. He knelt down in front of the whole court and begged his uncle

to change his mind.

'King Arthur was a wise king who loved Mordred dearly, so, after a little thought, he declared that cottage pie should be the favourite dish instead. Thousands of rabbits' lives were saved and cottage pie did become the preferred meal of the British people. The cleverest and bravest of all the rabbits wanted to thank Prince Mordred and so they took an oath to serve the Royal Family of England. They built a warren beneath the castle in Camelot and called themselves the Rabbits of the Round Table.'

'At the very moment that King Arthur freed the rabbits from the Curse of the Rabbit Pie, something magical happened, didn't it, Shylo?' said Horatio. 'Children and only children were given the ability to see those very special rabbits. But it is a gift that only lasts through childhood. As soon as they grow up, they lose that magic and see just ordinary rabbits, like everyone else.'

Shylo nodded, eager to continue. 'Many hundreds of years

later, when the Royal Family moved to London, the Rabbits of the Round Table became the Royal Rabbits of London. They built a vast warren beneath Buckingham Palace and continued to honour their oath.'

'Indeed,' Horatio interrupted, 'and they will never forget it. You see, without those brave Knights, the kings and queens of England wouldn't exist at all. They have no idea how hard those Royal Rabbits worked to protect them from danger.'

Shylo's one visible eye gleamed with fascination. 'You were going to tell me about the dogs . . . the Pack.'

Now Horatio's face grew very serious and his eyes flashed like knives in moonlight. Shylo thought that if any of his brothers and sisters could see the old rabbit now, they would faint with fear.

The old buck wiped his spectacles with a handkerchief. 'The Pack . . .' he said and his snarl sounded like ice cracking. 'Only one rabbit ever made it out of the Kennel alive ,' he said darkly. 'One clever buck, who was only seconds from death

. . . but *that* is another story. The others? Skins hanging on hooks. Dozens of them. Bowls full of rabbit tails; dishes full of rabbit paws. And the smell . . .'

His nostrils flared with distaste and Shylo thought of the most disgusting smell he knew, which was from a rotting pigeon killed by Tobias, and decided that the Kennel must stink even worse than that. He grimaced at the thought, for Shylo had an unusually sensitive nose.

Horatio replaced his spectacles and his eyes looked large and bloodshot behind the lenses. 'Those dogs can rip a rabbit's heart out with one snap of their teeth,' he added grimly and Shylo's knees knocked together. 'There are dangers in these forests, from prowling foxes and swooping kestrels, on the tracks from Range Rovers and tractors, and on the farm where Tobias hunts us and Farmer Ploughman's gun shoots us for his hotpot.'

Shylo shuddered at these words because his father had been killed by that gun when Shylo had been a tiny bunny and

he would always be scared of Farmer Ploughman now.

'But believe me,' Horatio continued, 'when I tell you that there's nothing that puts fear into the heart of a rabbit more than the yellow-fanged dogs of the Pack.'

Shylo was suddenly afraid because Horatio had switched from speaking about the past to the present. Surely the Royal Rabbits of London and the Pack had vanished in the mists of time? 'But they no longer exist, these dogs . . . do they?' His voice came out as a squeak.

Horatio saw that he had frightened the little bunny and was sorry. 'I think it's time you went home, young Shylo,' he said, patting his paw. 'I've got some more newspapers for you. Rabbits read so little these days, but all wisdom comes from reading.'

He handed Shylo a crumpled pile of newspapers and grinned crookedly. 'I stole them from the farm. That Tobias is a menace. Better watch out for him.'

'Thank you,' Shylo said, stuffing them under his arm.

'Now don't forget the turnips and try not to get caught on your way home.'

Shylo scampered back to the Warren as quickly as he could because his imagination had begun to conjure up snarling dogs behind every bush and tree.

CHAPTER TWO

When Shylo reached the Burrow, he scurried down the tunnel and gave the bag of turnips to his mother. She looked at the small sack of rotting vegetables and sighed.

'Oh, Shylo! Is this all you managed to find?'

Why, when all her other children were so quick and bouncy, was Shylo so utterly slow and clumsy? She loved her little one dearly, but every day she worried that he'd be eaten by a fox or lost in some piece of whirling farm machinery.

Shylo flopped on to a chair and pulled out the newspapers

Horatio had given him. This pleased his mother, for her other children never wanted to read anything, preferring noisy games instead.

Presently, Shylo's three brothers and three sisters arrived with sacks full of vegetables stolen from the farmer's fields, which made his little bag of turnips look very sorry indeed.

'Ha! Is that *all* the runt could manage?' cried his biggest brother, Maximilian, scornfully. Maximilian pulled Shylo's eyepatch then released it with a snap of elastic, causing his brother to squeal in pain.

'You're good for nothing, you are! I don't know why you bothered to get out of bed this morning!' And then Maximilian proceeded to leap round the room in great jumps and bounds to demonstrate how fit and athletic *he* was.

'Really, Maximilian, you're such a show-off,' laughed their mother. Shylo could see how proud she was of him and wished that he could jump and bound round the room like that, but all *he* could manage was a rather clumsy hop.

'Enough now, everybody,' she said. 'It's time for tea. Leave Shylo alone.'

'I can handle myself,' Shylo muttered as his siblings took their seats at the table and began to pile food on to their plates.

His mother straightened his patch. 'You won't have to wear this for long, dear,' she said kindly. 'Just until your eye gets stronger.'

Shylo wished he could tell his siblings about Horatio's story of the Pack. *That* would scare them, even Maximilian, who claimed not to be afraid of anything. But he knew he could never reveal his secret meetings with the old rabbit because he'd get into terrible trouble.

'Get some food in you,' his mother added. 'Parsnips will make you big and strong.' But the look on her face told him that she didn't believe it.

Shylo observed his siblings enviously. They were all glossy brown fur and fat white tails, long legs and stiff ears, and

extremely pleased with themselves. He imagined his mother must love them so much more than him. He climbed on to a chair and, with a helpless sniff, searched the almost empty dishes on the table for something to make him big and strong.

That night Shylo sat in the mouth of the tunnel leading into the Burrow and gazed up at the stars twinkling in the satin sky. He wished that he was clever and brave like the secret society of rabbits who had once lived beneath Buckingham Palace and protected the Royal Family of England from danger. He dreamed of a life of adventure. He longed to play a great part in Rabbit History, but he was afraid of getting hurt and being away from his mother.

He sighed. Maximilian was right: there was no rabbit weaker and more feeble than him. Even Shylo knew that his dreams were much too big for his little body.

The following morning, Shylo was shaken from sleep by Maximilian shouting in his ear. 'Shylo, get up! Rats have broken into the Warren! We have to get out NOW!'

Shylo's sister Blythe pulled back his duvet. 'Yes, now! Get up, get up!'

His two other sisters, Elvira and Erica, stood in the doorway, wringing their paws. 'Hurry or the rats will eat us all!'

Shylo leaped out of bed, but was so terrified that his knees buckled beneath him and he fell to the floor with a thud. Maximilian lifted him roughly on to his paws. 'Come on, Runt, or the rats will catch you!'

Shylo didn't waste time finding his clothes. He scampered through the Burrow in his pyjamas. As he charged through the kitchen, he knocked over the jug of carrot juice and it crashed to the ground. Plates went flying and chairs fell back. Desperate to flee the jaws of the fearsome rats, Shylo couldn't escape quickly enough. His heart beat so fast and so furiously he thought it might burst out of his chest.

When he reached the mouth of the Burrow, what did he see but Maximilian and his other siblings roaring with laughter. They were laughing so hard they had to hold their bellies.

'April Fool!' said Maximilian.

'And you're the biggest fool this April,' chimed his sisters in unison.

Shylo suddenly felt very silly in his pyjamas. Other rabbits hopped past on their way to the fields and he saw them giggling behind their paws. He tried to hold back the tears of hurt and embarrassment.

'Where's your sense of humour, Runt?' laughed Maximilian. 'It's only a joke.'

'Yes, it's only a joke,' repeated the others. 'Really, Shylo is no fun to be around!'

At breakfast, Mother noticed that Shylo was quieter than usual, but it wasn't until the evening, when he left the dinner

table early, complaining of a stomach ache, that she realized something was wrong. She found him tucked up in bed, although it wasn't nearly bedtime. She sat down beside him and stroked his forehead. 'What's the matter, Shylo?' she asked gently.

'Nothing,' he replied, not wanting to tell tales on his brothers and sisters. But he didn't have to. His mother knew, as all mothers do, and was sorry.

'You know, one day you'll show them,' she said, kissing him tenderly. 'One day you're going to make me very proud.'

Shylo opened his big brown eyes and a fat tear rolled down his face.

'I believe in you, Shylo,' she added. 'You just have to learn to believe in yourself.'

CHAPTER THREE

The following day, eager to hear more stories about the Royal Rabbits of London, Shylo pretended to his mother that he was going to the fields to steal a spring baby lettuce.

'Watch out for birds of prey,' she warned.

'He wouldn't make a very satisfying meal,' said Maximilian with a snigger and his other brothers and sisters sniggered with him.

Shylo couldn't leave the Burrow fast enough. He hopped up the tunnel and out into the fields at the edge of the forest, leaving the mocking sound of his siblings' laughter far behind

him. When he was sure he was alone, he lolloped into the trees.

As Shylo made his way further into the forest, the trees grew thicker and darker and it became eerily quiet. Then a twig snapped behind him and his heart leaped in his chest like a frantic cricket. He spun round in terror to find none other than Maximilian standing over him like a giant shadow.

'Where do you think you're going?' he demanded, rising up on his hind legs and folding his arms.

'None of your business,' Shylo replied, trying to sound brave.

'Oh, but it is, Runt. As your biggest brother, it's my duty to protect you. You shouldn't be in this part of the forest. It's dangerous.'

'I thought you'd be pleased if I got eaten by a fox.'

Maximilian narrowed his eyes. 'The fields are the other way, so you're not going there. Tell me, little brother, where *are* you going?'

Shylo shook his head, refusing to give his secret away. Maximilian reached out to grab his eyepatch, but, before he could, Shylo ducked and dashed into the undergrowth. He knew his brother was faster than him, but he also knew, from hiding from bullies his whole life, that being small could sometimes work to his advantage. With Maximilian at his heels, he zigzagged across the forest floor, jumping over branches and brambles, desperately searching for something low to dive under.

He stumbled on a tree stump and rolled like a bouncy ball down a small hill, *bounce-bounce-roly-poly*, until he came to an abrupt halt in a bank of nettles. He picked himself up and, trying to ignore his bruised and stinging bottom, limped on. With the blood pumping loudly in his ears, he searched for somewhere to hide. At last, he saw it: a fallen oak with a tiny gap beneath the great trunk, just small enough for him to wriggle into. With one last burst of energy, he threw himself beneath it.

Shylo squeezed his eyes tightly shut - but then he heard a squeaking and squealing noise. Barely daring to breathe, for fear of seeing Maximilian's big face glaring at him through the hole, he opened his eyes slowly.

One eye, of course, was hidden behind the red patch and only saw darkness, but the other made out only too well the source of the noise, and it wasn't Maximilian. Instead, through the gap beneath the trunk, Shylo saw a trio of big, greasy, menacing rats rubbing their pink paws together like thieves around a pot of gold. Maximilian had vanished, for not even he, with all his strength and vigour, could compete with a rat!

When they were very young, Shylo's father had given all his children the 'rat talk'.

'The world is full of rats,' Father Rabbit had explained. 'Country rats and city rats, uptown rats and downtown rats, rats in silvery dresses and diamonds, and rats with fleas in their fur. *All* of them are dangerous for rabbits!'

Luckily, Shylo had only encountered rats a few times in his

short life, but even *he* knew that this trio were no ordinary rats. No, indeed they were *not:* they were bigger, *much* bigger. Shylo thought they looked like *super*-rats! He shut his eyes again, hoping that when he opened them the rats would be gone, but it was no good. They were there in all their greasy, smelly horror and their squeaking made him shiver. It was almost too much, and yet Shylo found himself unable to look away.

The rats had cigarettes glued to their greenish lips, which let out whirls of bluish smoke, and they carried bulky cameras with giant long lenses over their shoulders. Their mobile phones were stashed in little leather pouches on belts around their waists and they wore headsets with small microphones placed in front of their mouths so that they could talk without dropping their cameras. Now they were squealing and wriggling round a tablet, which lit up their glistening pink snouts in the glare of its blue, flickering light.

Most rabbits would have run home to their mother,

especially ones as timid as Shylo, but he stayed put,
listening with mounting curiosity, even though he was in grave
danger . . .

What were the rats gazing at on the tablet screen and why
were they looking so pleased with themselves?

CHAPTER FOUR

The three rats hadn't noticed Shylo. He remained hidden beneath the trunk of the oak tree, trying to be as quiet as possible. He decided that in the event of the rats discovering him he would play dead. He knew what dead animals looked like and he was sure that if he lay still, and let his tongue hang out, he'd make a very convincing rabbit corpse.

From where he crouched, he could see them quite clearly. And he could smell them too because all rats smelled disgusting! Right now, Shylo wished that his sensitive nose was not quite so efficient. Their revolting pong reached him

like a sour fog and he had to concentrate very hard in order not to choke on it.

But wait! They were squeaking and he could hear what they were saying!

'A picture of the Queen in her bedroom without her crown would make every front page of every newspaper in the whole wide world!' said the fattest and greasiest rat, not bothering to wipe the long dribble of bright emerald-green snot that swung from his pink nostril.

The Queen! thought Shylo.

Now you may not know this, but whenever a rabbit hears the words *the Queen*, they sit up and use their ears to bow; even if they're in bed or on the run, rabbits always bow their ears for the Queen. So now, trapped as he was under the tree trunk, Shylo bowed his ears.

Her Majesty! In her bedroom? Without her crown! What a terrible thing!

'Yeah, Baz!' sniggered the shortest rat, rubbing his sticky

paws together gleefully. 'How about in her *nightie?* How much would that fetch us, eh?'

'In her nightie, Splodge!' guffawed the one with sticking-out teeth, an elongated, scraggy neck and a rather stupid expression on his face. 'I *like* it! In her *nightie!*'

The Queen in her nightie! Shylo didn't know whether to salute or bow or shout out in horror, he was so shocked by the rats' horrible plan.

'In her bedroom, in her nightie!' chortled Baz, letting the dribble of snot dangle dangerously close to the camera that was hanging around his neck.

'Yeah, Baz. No one's done that before! Now we've discovered a map that reveals a secret tunnel into her bedroom, it shouldn't be too difficult. Once we've taken the picture, we'll sell it for absolutely loads to the website that pays the most: *Rat-on-a-celebrity.com!*'

'For a million quid!' Baz sniffed loudly and the dribble of snot shot back into his nostril like a home-loving snake. 'Papa

Ratzi will be very pleased with us.'

'Very pleased,' agreed Splodge. 'A million quid is a fortune!'

'An absolute fortune,' Baz repeated, 'eh, Grimbo?'

'Yeah! We'll be *rich!*' said the scraggy-necked rat, who gave a little dance, wiggling his wrinkled bottom and waving his thick tail, finally lifting it up and letting out a noisy fart, which was so smelly it made Shylo gag.

Shylo, knowing it was only a matter of seconds before he erupted into a spasm of coughing and spluttering because of the stench, slunk back into the shadows. He found an exit on the other side of his hiding place and crept through it. He ran as fast as he could to Horatio's burrow. Somebody had to do something to stop the three rats, and fast!

'Ah,' said the old buck when Shylo tumbled into his sitting room without thumping his paw. 'Shylo Tawny-Tail in a hurry to hear more stories!' and he went to the bookshelf to take down *The Rise and Fall of the Great Rabbit Empire.*

The little rabbit staggered to his feet. 'No books! This time

it's real!' and out came the story in a breathless torrent of stammering: 'Rats . . . plot . . . Queen . . . bedroom . . . nightie!'

Horatio could not help bowing with his one good ear at the mention of Her Majesty, but his face darkened. 'What did you say?'

'Rats . . . plot . . . Queen . . . secret tunnel . . . nightie,' Shylo spluttered, catching his breath.

'Rats?' Horatio whispered. Shylo was too terrified to notice the old buck shudder. Horatio banged the book down on the table and hobbled slowly towards the bunny, leaning heavily on his walking stick. 'Take a deep breath, Shylo, and tell me exactly what you saw. These rats, what were they like?'

He placed a paw on Shylo's shoulder and the little bunny immediately felt encouraged. Horatio had never mocked him, or taunted him, or made fun of him. He was a rabbit who was very eager to hear what Shylo had to say. So Shylo took a deep breath, drew back his shoulders and

told Horatio about the conversation he had overheard in the forest.

When Shylo had finished, the old buck nodded thoughtfully. 'We don't have much time,' he growled. 'It sounds to me like you stumbled across a gang of Ratzis!'

'A what?' Shylo asked, confused.

'A gang of Ratzis. We haven't yet reached them in the book, but they're among the worst enemies the Royal Family have ever faced. Ratzis hunt them in order to make money from taking the most private photos of them, which they then sell, exposing those poor people to the world!'

At this, he went to the table and opened the book they had been looking at just a couple of days before.

'Here's a description of a Ratzi. Is this what they looked like?'

Shylo gazed down at the page and this is what he saw . . .

HOW TO SPOT A RATZI!

Very high squeaking voices.

Shiny fur glistening with grease (can be black or brown or grey).

Thin, bony chests.

Long, swollen bellies (because they eat too much fast food and only drink beer).

Saggy bottoms (because they're really very unfit).

Very, very long, pink, hairless tails, which are thick at one end, thin at the other.

Sharp teeth, sharp claws, sharp vision and long, thin tongues.

Snotty noses and big ears full of yellow wax.

They stink of rubbish because their rucksacks are full of rotting junk food and they also fart a lot, so you can smell them coming!

They always carry a camera, a phone and a tablet to send their photographs, and wear headsets with small microphones placed in front of their mouths.

They are very ugly creatures indeed!

Shylo nodded. 'Yes! That's who they were! Ratzis!'

'Then we must tell the Royal Rabbits at once,' said Horatio.

'The Royal Rabbits of London?' Shylo gasped. 'But I thought they no longer existed. I thought they were history.'

'I know what you thought, but that doesn't change the facts. They exist all right, perhaps now a little tired and forgotten, but they're the only ones who can stop the Ratzis.' Horatio looked grave.

'Every man, woman, child and animal in the world, from the highest queen to the lowest field mouse, famous or unknown, has a private place that they keep in their heart. It's the only thing that we can truly call our own. But the Ratzis want to destroy that private place by taking intimate photographs and sending them round the world via the internet.

'You see, Shylo, the internet is sometimes a very dangerous thing. It can steal a person's soul. Human beings don't know this because really they're very ignorant creatures, but we rabbits have a deep understanding of the world that they

don't have. The Ratzis, Shylo Tawny-Tail, are Soul-Stealers!'

Shylo's teeth began to chatter: this was a lot for a bunkin like him to take in. 'So how are you going to tell the Royal Rabbits of London?'

Horatio once again put his paw on Shylo's thin, bony shoulder. 'Not me! *You* are going to tell them.'

Shylo thought he must have misheard, but Horatio continued: 'I . . . well . . . I'm much too old to travel to London,' he said uneasily, his eyes lowered. He hesitated, as if searching for an excuse. 'Once I was young and adventurous and bold, but now . . . No, Shylo, it has to be you.'

He looked the stunned bunny up and down. 'You're a rabbit who is always curious to discover new things - how would you like to go to London? To the Royal Rabbit Headquarters - The Grand Burrow — at Buckingham Palace.'

Shylo was still unable to speak. All he could manage was a loud gulp and a high-pitched squeak, which was meant to sound like *'Me?',* but came out as 'Eek!' Shylo didn't feel

brave at all. He was frightened and ever so slightly regretful — if he hadn't run away from Maximilian, he might never have stumbled across the Ratzis.

At last, he found his voice, thin and trembling though it was. '*London?*' he gasped.

'Yes, of course! You're the only one apart from me who knows that the Royal Rabbits exist. The only rabbit who can prevent the Ratzis from sneaking into the Queen's bedroom and taking the photograph that will steal a little of her soul. She can't defend herself: only the Royal Rabbits can do that. How shameless those Ratzis are! How *very, very* shameless.' Horatio shivered. 'Come on, you must leave at once!'

'But I'm not strong enough or . . . or . . . brave enough. My brothers and sisters call me Runt!'

Horatio smiled at him kindly. 'This is one of those moments that can change a rabbit's life forever — yes, even the weakest and most feeble! Do you remember the first time we met?

'You'd wandered over to my side of the forest and had

found some old newspapers I'd discarded among the bluebells. You sat down and started to read. I noticed how brave you were to venture into this forbidden part of the forest, but also how curious. It was your thirst for knowledge that impressed me the most. When I approached, you didn't scamper off. Do you remember what you said?'

Shylo shook his head.

'You said: "Why is everyone afraid of you?" You see, your curiosity made you brave. Shylo Tawny-Tail, you are braver than you know.'

'But how will I find the headquarters when I get to London?' Shylo asked.

'Listen carefully.' The excitement rose in Horatio's voice. 'I'll tell you exactly how to get there!'

Shylo, just for a moment, started to cry. 'I'll get lost!' he protested in a small voice.

'No, you won't. Now you're not crying, are you, Shylo?'

'Not any more,' Shylo replied with a sniff, lifting his chin.

'Good. I have great faith in you. As I always say: *Life is an adventure. Anything in the world is possible — by will and by luck, with a moist carrot, a wet nose and a slice of mad courage!* You're going to discover that there's more to you than you ever imagined.'

CHAPTER FIVE

Horatio shuffled towards the dresser and reached stiffly down to the bottom left-hand cupboard. Shylo thought he was going to open it. Instead, he turned the knob like the dial of a safe: once to the right, twice to the left, three times to the right, muttering to himself as he did so. Then he pulled, hard.

'Carrots and turnips! This thing was always very stiff,' Horatio grumbled. He gave the cupboard a kick and tried again, but the door still wouldn't open. 'Trouble is, it hasn't been used in years.'

He straightened up and looked at Shylo with a sniff. 'You try. Give it a good kick.'

Shylo banged the door with his paw, but Horatio was unimpressed. 'That wouldn't kill a fly! Give it a *proper* kick with your hind leg. Go on!'

Shylo turned round, squeezed his eyes shut and thrust his back paw against the wood. Horatio bent again and pulled the knob. To his satisfaction, the door opened with a creak.

'See this?' he said, leaning down. 'It's a secret tunnel which will take you to the barn on Farmer Ploughman's farm where the crates are packed up with vegetables for London and loaded on to a van. They're harvesting spring green cabbage at the moment, so you can hide among those. You're a small rabbit. No one's going to find you and, if they do, you must run.

'The main thing is to get to London. The farmer delivers to the poshest hotel there, right next to Green Park, a large field in the heart of the city that's full of rabbits. Go there and

find the Weeping Willow. Beneath the Weeping Willow, you will come across a Royal Rabbit.'

'But how will I even recognize a Royal Rabbit?' Shylo asked, his stomach beginning to churn with nerves at the thought of the adventure ahead.

'Oh, you'll know all right. First you'll see the Badge, the unmistakable red paint on the sole of one of their front paws, and second you'll see that they're not like other rabbits. They're . . .' Horatio hesitated and stroked his grey whiskers one by one. 'They're . . . knowing. Important. Busy-looking Hopster rabbits. Not like rabbits from the countryside.'

'But what do I say when I find one?'

'Listen carefully; this is important: when you recognize a member of the Royal Rabbits, you say: "I think it's going to rain rats and frogs."'

Shylo frowned. 'Rats and frogs?'

'Yes,' Horatio answered. 'You say: "I think it's going to rain rats and frogs." Then they will answer: "A thump of the paw

is as good as a carrot in the warren," and you'll know that they're a true Royal Rabbit.'

Shylo did his best to memorize the code phrase, but Horatio was already rushing ahead.

'Do *not* trust any rabbit who doesn't know the code. Once you're satisfied that you're talking to a genuine Royal Rabbit, you must demand to be taken to the Royal Rabbit with the Double Badge and only then, when you're face to face with *him*, can you tell him your name and the nature of your mission. Those are the Rabbit Rules of Secret Craft!'

Horatio patted Shylo on the back, then moved past him to the store cupboard.

Oh dear, thought Shylo nervously. He wouldn't remember ANY of that!

'Now I can't send you off without a snack for the journey,' Horatio added, picking up a dry-looking carrot and handing it to Shylo. 'Although I suspect you'll enjoy a grand feast of spring green cabbage on the way. Here's a torch for your

pocket. You'll be needing that for the tunnel. Hurry, you must catch the van before it leaves!'

'But I have to say goodbye to my mother!' cried Shylo.

For the first time, Horatio looked annoyed. 'Your mother?' he snapped. 'You can't tell your mother where you're going!'

Shylo's ears drooped again and he felt very small and silly. 'I need to let her know so she doesn't worry,' he explained in a shaky voice.

'Doesn't worry?' Horatio roared. 'Good greengage! There's a plot against the Queen . . .' (they both bowed their floppies) '. . . and you're worrying about your mother? Shylo Tawny-Tail, you are just about to head off on an adventure! You'll leave as the scrawniest runt of her litter, but will return a big, brave buck and make her proud.'

If I return at all, thought Shylo, fighting back tears. 'Am I to go alone?' he asked, almost wishing that he was allowed to take one of his brothers. Now more than ever he longed to be like Maximilian. His biggest brother would rise to the

challenge and probably save the Queen single-handedly (and boast about it shamelessly for months . . .).

'Of course you must go alone. You can't tell anyone about your mission, do you understand? You have to find the Royal Rabbits of London and repeat what you overheard or the Queen will be harmed. Go! By will and by luck, with a moist carrot, a wet nose and a slice of mad courage!'

'By will and by luck, with a moist carrot, a wet nose and a slice of mad courage,' repeated Shylo with a thumping heart.

And so it was that the runt of the litter, the weakest and most feeble of all the rabbits in the Warren, the butt of his siblings' jokes and mocking laughter, shone his torch into the dark tunnel and made his way slowly into the unknown.

CHAPTER SIX

With a carrot to sustain him and only a drop of courage, Shylo left Horatio's warm burrow behind and hopped anxiously along the muddy tunnel, deep underground.

The thought of what dangers might be lurking in a tunnel that hadn't been used in years rose in his mind and made his teeth chatter. What if he got tangled in electrical wires or bumped into a weasel? He had nothing but his claws to protect himself with and they weren't even sharp enough to cut through a turnip. If he met a badger, with its crushing jaws, his mission would be over before it had started.

With all these worries weighing down on him, Shylo soon began to think about turning back. He'd explain to Horatio that he wasn't the right rabbit for the job.

Suddenly, he heard a rustling further along the tunnel and froze. *It won't take me long to return to Horatio's burrow if I run as fast as I can*, he thought. But then Shylo remembered his mother telling him to eat more parsnips so he'd grow to be big and strong; and Horatio telling him that there was more to him than he could ever imagine; and the desire to be brave rose in him like a great tide. It pushed him on towards the rustling, as if he was not a runt at all but a brave Knight of the Crown, a Spy of the Rabbit Rules of Secret Craft.

To his relief, the rustling turned out to be nothing more than a leaf blowing in the wind that swept down the tunnel from the opening that at last came into view in a blaze of natural light. He switched off his torch and leaped towards the hole with a rush of excitement. He'd done it. He'd made it to the farm.

Shylo peeped out of the hole and looked around. He had come out beside a big green barn. He turned his eyes to the field behind him, which rose towards the forest in a gentle slope, and knew that Horatio's burrow was just up there, hidden beneath the bracken. He wondered whether the old buck was watching him. That thought gave him an extra boost of courage.

He hopped out and poked his head into the barn.

It was exactly as Horatio had said. The fat farmer's wife was busy packing cabbages into crates while her ruddy-faced husband lifted the full ones into the back of a van, which had been reversed into the barn. They were chatting happily as they worked, half listening to the radio on a table against the wall.

In the workshop at the back, Shylo could see their son and daughter through a large glass window. They were sitting on a sofa, playing a computer game, staring with dead eyes at the TV screen as if in a trance.

Shylo had to think fast. He could see that the farmer's wife was about to finish packing the cabbages. He imagined that, once the last crate had been loaded into the van, the doors would close and the opportunity to jump in would be lost. Frantically, he scanned the room. There had to be some way to distract the farmer and his wife. Shylo had survived the tunnel without turning back; he was *not* going to fail now.

Then he had an idea. It was a brave idea, braver than any he'd ever had before and he didn't have time to think it through. If he had, he probably wouldn't have had the courage to do it.

He slunk into the barn and hopped along the edge of the wall, like he'd seen the farm cat do a thousand times when he had defied his mother and sneaked away to steal the farmer's vegetables or simply to observe the human world which fascinated him so much.

Once he reached the back wall, he jumped on to a container, then from the container on to a cardboard box, then from

the cardboard box on to a shelf laden with greasy bottles whose stained labels spelled out the words **RAT POISON** in red, beneath a picture of a skull and crossbones. Shylo shuddered, trying not to brush up against any of them . . .

From there, he squeezed through the window, which was open a crack, into the workshop where the children were staring at the TV screen. They didn't see him; they were so focused on their game that they wouldn't have noticed if an elephant had charged into the room! Shylo hopped on to the floor and followed the trail of wire from the computer to the wall. Then he put his paw on the plug, as he had seen the farmer do, and switched it off.

The reaction was instant. The children started shouting: 'Mum, Dad! The Xbox has gone off! We're in the middle of our game! Dad, do something!'

You might have thought the house was on fire as both parents stopped what they were doing and looked at each other in alarm. *This* was enormously satisfying to a small

rabbit who had been taunted by his siblings all his life for being cowardly.

'What on earth?' cried Mrs Ploughman. 'Quick! We have to turn the computer back on or the children will scream the house down!'

The farmer ran into the workshop, followed by his wife, leaving the door wide open. Shylo only had a moment to escape and dash across the barn floor to the open doors of the van. With a great leap, he lunged towards it. But the little rabbit didn't make it. He clung to the edge with his front paws while his hind legs pedalled furiously in mid-air, and he tried desperately to scramble inside. He hoped Tobias the cat didn't spot his paddling legs.

'Who did that then? A ghost?' Mrs Ploughman asked when her husband had turned the plug back on and the children had fallen silent again.

'Dunno. Mighty strange, if you ask me. There's no one here but us. It appears to have switched off all by itself.'

'Must be the cat,' she suggested.

'I can't see no cat.' He looked under the table. 'Tobias, is that you?' Bewildered, Mr and Mrs Ploughman walked back into the barn, closing the workshop door behind them so that their children could play their game in peace.

'There, last cabbage,' said Mrs Ploughman with a sigh, plonking it into the crate. 'I think it's time for a cup of tea. How 'bout you?'

'No time for that. Got to get myself to London.'

The farmer lifted the final crate. Shylo, foaming at the mouth with fear and exhaustion, gave one last, frantic kick and heaved himself inside the van. Farmer Ploughman was so busy thinking about his journey that he didn't see the little rabbit lying panting beside the crates and dropped the last one on to the floor of the van. He narrowly missed squashing Shylo who was now almost completely wedged between the boxes of spring cabbage. The van doors closed and the interior was plunged into darkness.

Shylo lay a while, listening to his heart thumping like the beat of a drum. Little by little, it grew slower and quieter until it ticked in the usual way, like a regular clock. As the excitement and fear subsided and the engine began to roar, followed by the gentle vibration of the wheels, Shylo realized that he was on his way to London. There was no turning back.

He sat up and gazed forlornly at the sealed doors of the van. He wished there was a window so he could see the farm for the last time. He wished he'd been able to say goodbye to his mother and he wondered if he was doing the right thing. But then he felt a swell of something unexpected in his chest: he'd made it down the tunnel, reached the farm and managed to climb into the van. How proud Horatio would be! How proud Shylo was of himself!

All that excitement had made the little rabbit hungry. He squeezed through a hole in a crate and inhaled the sweet smell of spring cabbage. Then he took a bite. Never in his life had he tasted anything so delicious. When this was all over

and he came home, Shylo decided he'd bring his mother the biggest spring cabbage he could find.

CHAPTER SEVEN

Shylo awoke to the sound of voices. He sprang up, heart racing, and dived into a crate to hide beneath the cabbages. The big doors opened and the back of the van was flooded with light. He began to tremble with fear, which made the cabbages tremble too. He shrank down deeper, hoping the farmer wouldn't notice.

'Sorry I'm late. I hit a bit of traffic,' said Farmer Ploughman, lifting the crate — and Shylo — out of the van.

Shylo barely dared open his good eye. The swaying motion made him feel sick and he wished he hadn't eaten so many

cabbages. Through the slats of the crate he could see the van was parked in a small street between huge towering buildings — *These must be hotels*, Shylo thought — and across a roaring, busy road was the green foliage of a park. If Horatio was right about where the van was supposed to drop the cabbages off in London then that must be Green Park!

The crate was dropped on to the ground with a thud. Shylo froze. *Now what?* But, before he could work out his next move, a dark shadow cut out the light as another crate was being lowered on top of him. Afraid of being trapped, he shot out of his hiding place and scampered off as fast as he could to seek shelter.

'Eh, did you see that?' a woman screeched. 'It was a rabbit!' She cackled like an old witch. 'You brought more than cabbages up from the country!'

'A rabbit?' the farmer exclaimed. 'Are you sure?'

'I know a rabbit when I see one. A brown one, it was. Small and skinny. Nothing to it.'

'Where did it go then?'

'Under that car. What are you going to do?'

Farmer Ploughman knelt down and looked behind the wheel where Shylo cowered. 'Catch it and give it to my wife for the pot.'

'But it's got no meat on it at all. Better to give it to the dog.'

'Hey, little rabbit, don't be frightened. I'm not going to hurt you.' The farmer reached under the car. 'Hey,' he hissed at the woman. 'Come over here and give me a hand. I've nearly got him.'

Shylo saw the farmer's hand to his right, and the woman's hand to his left, and didn't wait for their grasping fingers to close round him. He did not intend for his mission to end in a pot of stew or in the jaws of a dog.

He scooted out from under the car and ran clumsily down the little road towards the park, but, as he drew closer, he could see that the rushing London traffic on the big road was between him and those green meadows! He prayed to the

Great Rabbit in the sky that he wouldn't trip or stumble or get squashed beneath a lorry. How was he going to get across? Nothing could have prepared Shylo for the London streets. On grey, filthy paving stones he saw thousands of walking feet. When he looked up, he realized that most of the humans had phones clamped to their ears or were just staring at the little screens, scarcely noticing anything around them.

There were bollards and traffic lights, signposts and dustbins, and the noise. Oh, the noise! The thunder of the cars and lorries, the whizzing of wheels and the roaring of angry engines were all deafening for poor Shylo. And the smell! For a little rabbit with an extremely sensitive nose, the stench was nearly as bad as the Ratzis!

Woof-woof-grrr! A dog, a Golden Retriever, lunged at Shylo with a snarl. The poor little rabbit hopped backwards in terror, but the dog couldn't reach him: it was on a leash and its owner hadn't even noticed — she was too busy messaging on her phone. Then, suddenly, there came another

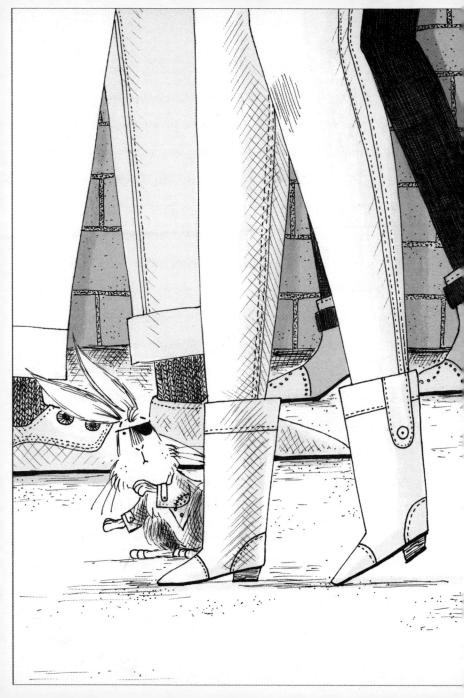

woof-woof-grrr!: this time a snapping terrier. Shylo froze. But this dog was also on a lead and it was quickly dragged off down a tunnel that seemed to go under the road.

Shylo thought of his home — the quiet Northamptonshire fields, the warm comfort of his mother's kitchen, the butterflies and bees in summer, the sun setting over golden crops of wheat and barley — and he longed to be back there with every fibre of his being.

It isn't supposed to end like this, he thought glumly, but this task had always been too much for a feeble rabbit like him. He imagined how disappointed Horatio would be. How a fragment of the Queen's soul would be snatched by the Ratzis. How his mother would shake her head and his brothers and sisters would laugh at his tragic end.

And how utterly and pathetically predictable his failure would be.

But then, just as he was about to give up he heard Horatio's familiar voice as if he was right beside him: *'You might be frail,*

Shylo Tawny-Tail, but never waste time worrying about things you can't change! You're cleverer than you realize. Learn from your enemies!'

Shylo turned back to those frightening dogs and saw that the tunnel their owners had taken them through did run under the road and into the park: Instead of running away, he followed them. His heart filled with hope as he leaped down the steps and scurried quickly along the tunnel, keeping to the shadows. When he emerged at the other end, the smell of freshly cut grass and the whisper of leaves on the trees restored his flagging courage.

He headed further into the park, which was almost like the countryside with its swathes of purple crocuses and yellow daffodils. He took shelter beneath a bush and little by little his breathing grew regular and his heartbeat slowed.

It was hard to believe that he'd been in the Warren that morning. Home felt very far away. As Shylo reflected on his adventure, he began to swell with pride. He'd succeeded where

everyone would have expected him to fail. Perhaps he was the right rabbit for the job, after all.

He spotted a squirrel greedily munching on a packet of biscuits she'd just dragged out of a bin. Shylo decided to be brave and ask the squirrel if she knew anything about the Weeping Willow.

The squirrel looked at him hard. 'Are you a tourist?'

Shylo was afraid to admit that, so said nothing.

The squirrel took pity on him. 'You're not from around here, are you? Look, it's not far. Come on, I'll take you myself. Human tourists love feeding squirrels and there are always lots of those by the willow.'

She led Shylo along winding pathways, through the luscious, damp grass, until he started to wonder if the squirrel knew where she was going. But eventually the little animal raised her eyes to the sky.

Shylo looked up. There, rustling above him in the gentle breeze, were the elegant branches of a weeping willow.

The Weeping Willow, framed by a beautiful rosy orange glow as London's sky was tinged with the beginnings of dusk. Shylo opened his mouth to thank the squirrel, but she'd gone, chasing after a group of tourists carrying paper bags bulging with food.

CHAPTER EIGHT

Shylo noticed a scruffy-looking brown rabbit nibbling on a patch of grass near the trunk of the Weeping Willow. In his rush to carry out his plan, he forgot everything Horatio had told him and hopped over nervously. The rabbit stopped chewing and gazed at him dumbly.

Shylo looked around to make sure they wouldn't be overheard. Then he sidled up and whispered: 'I think it's going to rain rats and frogs.'

'Oy, keep ya distance!' The brown rabbit looked at him blankly. 'What's that you've got on yer eye?'

Shylo was surprised. He'd expected the little animal to come out with the secret reply: *A thump of the paw is as good as a carrot in the warren.* So he repeated what Horatio had taught him, this time a little louder.

'I THINK IT'S GOING TO RAIN RATS AND FROGS!'

'No, it ain't,' said the rabbit, chewing again and scratching himself. 'And I don't like talking to strangers, so hop it!'

Shylo waited for something more to happen, but the rabbit feasted on, ignoring Shylo, until eventually he huffily lolloped off and disappeared into a bush.

Shylo was left feeling frustrated and anxious. As the brown rabbit had hopped away, he'd noticed that there was no red sole to his front paw. He was quite obviously not a member of the Royal Rabbits and Shylo felt foolish for having mistaken him for one. How could he have forgotten the Rabbit Rules of Secret Craft already? The little bunny sat by the trunk of the Weeping Willow and waited.

And waited.

And then waited some more.

Rabbits came and went, but none looked any different from the brown rabbit Shylo had spoken to and he began to lose hope. His stomach was rumbling. He nibbled on a blade of grass, which tasted bitter and not at all like country grass, and wondered whether he was ever going to find a member of the mysterious Royal Rabbits.

Then he began to lose faith in Horatio. Perhaps the Leaders of the Warren were right after all and the old buck *was* mad. Perhaps he'd made all those stories up, like the Rabbits of the Round Table. Perhaps the Royal Rabbits of London didn't exist at all. Shylo felt foolish for having believed him. How his brothers and sisters would howl with laughter if they could see him now!

The park grew dark. Shylo imagined it was full of city foxes, owls and rats who would love to dine on a young skinny bunkin, in spite of what his mean siblings said, and he worried about where he was going to spend the night.

Just then, a very suave, sleek and handsome rabbit with short grey hair, long, black-tipped ears and an intelligent, alert expression hopped out from under the famous willow tree. In the grainy dusk, Shylo could see that the rabbit was wearing well-pressed black trousers, a dashing black dinner jacket and a scarlet bow tie. He had the air of a rabbit of the world. Was this what Horatio had called a Hopster rabbit?

Shylo stopped worrying and stood on his hind legs. The Hopster rabbit gave him a tough, no-nonsense stare, but said nothing. He began to look around as if searching for something.

Well, Shylo thought to himself, *he certainly looks knowing, important and busy-looking.*

Hastily gathering his courage, he lolloped over to the Hopster rabbit who was so tall he didn't see the little bunny at his feet until he heard him sneeze.

The rabbit glanced down at Shylo in distaste. 'Oh really, how very uncouth,' he said.

Shylo wiped his nose and the tall rabbit hopped away.

Suddenly, Shylo saw a flash of red paw in the gloom. *The Badge!*

'I think . . .' he began, hurrying after the Hopster, desperate not to lose him. 'I think it's going to rain rats and frogs,' he blurted as darkness was about to swallow the rabbit.

A moment later, two shiny black eyes appeared, then long, black-tipped ears, a grey head and a surprised expression.

'*What* did you just say?' demanded the Hopster.

'I . . . I think it's going to rain rats and frogs.'

The tall rabbit came closer. He bent down and put his face a few centimetres from Shylo's. His nose twitched. He frowned. 'A thump of the paw is as good as a carrot in the warren. What's your name?' he asked.

'No names,' Shylo stammered. 'Rabbit Rules of Secret Craft.'

'Why are you here?' demanded the rabbit briskly.

'I only report my name and mission to the Royal Rabbit with the double Badges,' Shylo replied a little more bravely, remembering what Horatio had told him.

The Hopster rabbit smiled grimly. 'Well done. You do know where you are, don't you?' He parted the branches of the Weeping Willow and finally Shylo saw it. Rising up like a giant white cake and magnificent in the golden rays of sunset, was Buckingham Palace, and beneath it somewhere, was the Royal Rabbit Headquarters.

The Union Jack fluttered high above the palace, which Shylo knew meant that the monarch was at home. The little bunny remained awestruck for a moment. He'd seen pictures of this in the newspapers Horatio collected, but to clap eyes on it in real life was something else altogether. It was spectacular, truly spectacular, and Shylo couldn't help saluting with his ears, giving the Queen a double-flopsy.

Then his stomach began to churn with nerves. The Ratzis could be on their way already!

'You'd better come with me,' said the big rabbit quietly and Shylo nodded.

'Stay close; don't make a sound.'

CHAPTER NINE

The red-pawed rabbit looked around, checking they weren't being followed. Then he parted the branches of the Weeping Willow: 'Get in!' he ordered.

It was dark in there and smelled of damp earth, and for a moment it reminded Shylo of the warren and he felt a stab of homesickness. But there was no time to think of that. The Hopster rabbit thumped the ground a few times with his hind paw and Shylo felt the vibrations course through his body, for this big buck was really very large and extremely strong.

'Who twitches there?' came a high-pitched voice out of a

speaker hidden in the earth.

'Clooney,' the rabbit replied. 'We have a visitor.'

There was a brief pause. 'A visitor?'

'He used the *old* code.'

'What do you mean, the *old* code?' asked the voice. 'We have passwords now and they're changed every year . . .'

'Rats and frogs.'

'Rats and frogs! But that's . . .'

'The *old* code, when there *were* codes. Long before our time,' said Clooney impatiently. 'Now let us in at once!'

'All right, all right, don't raise your voice at *me*.'

The turf fell away and revealed a manhole cover, which sprang open like a trapdoor. Under a spaghetti-like tangle of multicoloured wires hidden beneath the opening, Shylo saw an ordinary little rabbit hole. Oh, how that made him think of the Burrow and his mother's home-nibbled carrots! But again he had no time to dwell on that because Clooney grabbed him and pushed him into the hole where Shylo found himself at

once sliding swiftly down a chute like a slide at a swimming pool. He landed with a bump and came to an abrupt halt on a red gym mat, followed by Clooney, who landed nimbly on his shiny black shoes.

The big rabbit lifted Shylo to his paws, brushed him down and murred: 'Right. You're in. Now we need answers.'

For a moment, Shylo's fear turned to awe and he gazed about in wonder. He was in a tunnel which opened out into an enormous hallway with a vaulted ceiling. Bright wall lights on either side lit up a line of train tracks and a cart. He had made it to The Grand Burrow and he couldn't believe he'd done it!

Just then, a plump female rabbit in a red-and-gold ceremonial uniform appeared before him, holding a long, bejewelled staff.

'Welcome, whoever you are. My name is Frisby,' she said in a very *fluffily-buffily* voice. 'I am the Major-domo of the Palace, which means I run everything down here. Without me, the pencils don't get sharpened, the dinner doesn't get served

and the Paws of the Household would do no work at all.'

'Stop rabbiting on, Frisby,' said Clooney. The handsome rabbit rubbed his chin, narrowed his eyes and gave the little bunkin a long, hard stare. 'This is a job for the Marshal of the Thumpers. We need to find out who this little rabbit is and fast,' he muttered to himself.

Without further ado, he tossed Shylo into the cart and jumped in after him. Frisby climbed in behind them and pressed a well-worn red button on the dashboard and the cart set off down the track with a jerk.

Clooney didn't speak to Shylo. He seemed distracted, but then Shylo noticed that the beautifully groomed rabbit was admiring his own reflection in the glass and muttering with a satisfied smile: 'I am sooo handsome.' Frisby observed Shylo carefully, staring curiously at his eyepatch. Shylo looked ahead, waiting for the track to come to an end as the wind raked through his fur with cold fingers.

At last, the cart stopped. Clooney hopped off on to

a carpet, which was a rich, royal scarlet, but stained and covered with holes. He made for a round door built into the earth and punched a code into a large, clunky keypad beside it. The door shook and then opened with a breezy sound like an *Oooh!*

Shylo followed Clooney into a massive hall, far bigger than the size of the entire Warren back home, and his jaw swung open in astonishment. Horatio's stories hadn't prepared him for this.

There were many levels, built round a large, circular hall, adorned with a giant but very cobwebby chandelier. As he looked up, Shylo could see different floors connected by wooden stairways, all busy with the comings and goings of hard-working rabbits, walking on their hind legs.

The does wore old-fashioned blue uniforms consisting of a jacket and skirt, and the bucks wore blue trousers and ties. They were full of activity: busy at their desks, talking around tables, hopping up and down the winding staircases,

carrying papers, folders, document bags and cartons of carrot juice. Shylo didn't know what they were all doing, but it looked very important.

They worked on old-fashioned, clunky typewriters which went *click-click-clickety-click*; Shylo could hear the *tring-tring* of old telephones and, with his highly sensitive nose, he could detect the smell of ancient, dusty books and (less appealing) the musty smell of sweat. It reminded him of home, when the whole family had spent a winter's day underground.

Three rabbits in red tailcoats with ruffs and gold buttons stepped forward. 'Good morning, sir,' said one. 'Welcome. I am the duty Master of the Paw and it's my job to make sure that you're comfortable. Do you have a suitcase or–'

Clooney, ever suave, sleek and handsome, cut him off briskly. 'Just get me the phone,' he commanded. 'I need the hotline.'

A young doe in a blue coat with gold buttons rushed over, carrying a silver plate with an ancient black telephone balanced

on top of it. Clooney lifted the telephone and dialled a long number. 'It's the Groom of the Tail here. Tell the Marshal of the Thumpers we have a visitor.'

He looked down at Shylo and added: 'He doesn't look like much but I suggest the Marshal comes at once. Tell him the visitor knows the *old* code.'

CHAPTER TEN

No sooner had Clooney put down the telephone than a very large black Hopster rabbit appeared at the bottom of the staircase, followed by a squad of fierce-looking Thumpers, whom Shylo imagined were the Special Forces unit of highly trained soldier rabbits. The leader was not as tall as Clooney, but he was the strongest-looking rabbit that Shylo had ever seen and the whole room seemed to step aside to let him pass.

'Morning, Monsters! You called the Marshal?' said the black Hopster in a loud, deep voice with a strong Jamaican

accent. It resounded off the chandelier and echoed up the stairway. 'Well, here I am! We have a security problem? You need muscle? Sounds like a job for Zeno.'

His fur was shaved so that you could see his huge muscles gleaming and bulging and rippling as he walked, and his thighs alone were wider than Shylo's entire body. When he arrived, Clooney saluted with one ear.

'So who's the pirate?' Zeno asked and Shylo shrank behind Clooney.

'He said the *old* code,' Clooney informed him. 'I had no choice but to bring him in.'

'Rats and frogs?' said Zeno in surprise. He narrowed his eyes and peered at Shylo, who winced. 'And you brought him into the heart of The Grand Burrow?'

Clooney laughed. 'You really think this poor excuse for a rabbit is going to be a threat to us?'

'PERHAPS HE'S NOT ALONE!' shouted Zeno with such a loud boom that it echoed twice round the chamber, which was

so quiet you could have heard a dandelion drop. 'Sounds like something Papa Ratzi might have cooked up. Are you working for Papa Ratzi? Have you brought the Ratzis into . . .'

'Unless he's a kangaroo in disguise with an army of rats in his pouch, he's very much alone,' said Clooney calmly.

'OK, let's take him into the library and hear what he has to say,' thundered the muscly rabbit. Accompanied by two large Thumpers, Clooney and Zeno, Shylo was escorted into a circular room containing a round table, twelve chairs and countless shelves of dusty old books that made Shylo think of Horatio.

'So what do you have to tell me?' asked Zeno.

'I . . . I . . . I overheard a plot against the Queen,' Shylo declared in a small voice, then he remembered that Horatio had told him not to discuss his mission with anyone but the rabbit with two red paws. Zeno only had *one*.

They all bowed with their ears at the mention of the Queen.

'Sure you did,' said Zeno, sounding unconvinced.

'I . . . I . . . did,' Shylo squeaked.

Zeno bared his teeth. 'What are you *really* here for?'

Shylo cowered in fear. He wanted to make himself so small as to disappear altogether.

'What's all the fuss about?' said a female voice with a strong French accent. The Thumpers parted and in she came, as grand as a countess, in a flouncy scarlet dress.

Shylo found himself looking into the coffee-coloured eyes of a sleek, pale-brown doe with a full, curvy body and he was momentarily mesmerized like a mouse before a snake. She was more beautiful than any rabbit he had ever seen.

Suddenly, he was aware of how dirty he must look after his journey.

'May I present Belle de Paw,' said Zeno. 'Doe of the Dressing Table.'

As you might imagine from the title, Belle de Paw was responsible for looking after the security of the Queen's bedroom. However, what you might *not* imagine is how often

her quick little paws pinched the odd diamond, crown jewel or trinket, like Queen Victoria's thimbles that the present Queen liked to display on her dressing table. Indeed, Belle de Paw's burrow truly twinkled and sparkled with the many gems she had most dishonestly acquired.

Belle de Paw ran her bejewelled claws over the glittering diamond collar about her neck and smiled at the terrified rabbit. 'So who are you, little bunny?' she asked.

'Shylo Tawny-Tail,' he replied, straightening up.

'He said the *old* code,' Zeno informed her gravely.

'*That* hasn't been used for years,' she gasped. 'How do you know it, little rabbit? Who gave it to you?' She narrowed her eyes suspiciously. 'How like the Ratzis to use a one-eyed bunkin to sneak inside.'

'*Hora– Hora–*' Shylo was desperate to convince them that he was telling the truth, but the word 'Horatio' formed a sticky ball on his tongue.

Belle de Paw interrupted him and rounded on Clooney.

'How irresponsible of you to bring a stranger into headquarters! What if he has endangered our organization? *Zut alors!* What if the Ratzis break in? We will have to flee. But we cannot leave. We have nowhere to go.'

She threw her paws up at the Thumpers, flashing large, sparkling rings. 'I couldn't possibly pack all my jewels and my pretty clothes! I cannot exist without *mes diamants!*' She stared at Zeno with desperate eyes. 'Well, you muscle-bound *idiot*, DO something!'

Zeno rolled his eyes because Belle de Paw always thought of herself first, but he was just as curious to hear the bunkin's tale as she was. 'Tell us about this plan to harm the Queen,' he demanded.

Shylo was so afraid that all he could muster was a weak murr: 'I can't say any more until I see the Royal Rabbit with Two Badges. Rabbit Rules of Secret Craft!'

Zeno looked at Belle de Paw, who looked at Clooney, who in turn looked at Shylo. Zeno shrugged. 'He's right. Rabbit

Rules. We must take him to meet the Generalissimo.'

And in that moment, when those knowing, important and busy-looking Hopster rabbits did as he asked, Shylo felt as if he was the bravest country bunny that had ever hopped the Earth.

But who was the Generalissimo and would he believe Shylo's story?

CHAPTER ELEVEN

Zeno, Clooney and Belle de Paw led Shylo through a large door at the other end of the hall and up a winding staircase. Shylo wished Horatio had come with him. He would know what to do. Shylo shivered beneath his fur and felt very tired and hungry.

They arrived at a pair of tall double doors, guarded on either side by a Hopster rabbit in a scarlet coat. The rabbits pushed open the doors and Shylo found himself in a small anteroom where groups of rabbits sat waiting on crimson chairs, whispering quietly.

Frisby, the Major-domo whom Shylo had met when he first arrived, was standing in the middle of the room. She twitched her nose suspiciously at the sight of Shylo, but, on seeing that he was accompanied by Zeno, Clooney and Belle de Paw, she nodded at the big Thumpers standing guard outside another pair of double doors and hopped over to knock three times with her staff. The doors opened slowly.

Shylo peered inside and saw an old grey rabbit, in a plain green uniform and military boots, bending over a long table, studying a map of London. Beside it was a model of Buckingham Palace made of matchsticks — Shylo thought it must have taken years to make! Rabbits with little rakes moved markers round the map while others sat at desks, talking on old-fashioned black telephones.

A chocolate-coloured doe with short, spiky hair and gleaming blue eyes was giving instructions to the rabbits round the map. Shylo was transfixed by the flamboyant colours of the American flag dyed on her arms: one arm was red and

white stripes, the other white stars on blue. The belt that hung around her hips was loaded with ropes, knives and a large black whip.

When she saw them enter, she tapped the old grey rabbit on the shoulder. 'We got company, Generalissimo,' she said with an American accent.

'Thank you, Laser.' He looked at the group now standing before him. 'Zeno? Belle de Paw, Clooney? Report!' he ordered.

His voice was clipped, gravelly and commanded respect. The Generalissimo had once been tall like Zeno and Clooney, but age had caused his shoulders to hunch and his back to curve. His face was thin, his whiskers white, his grey fur short and prickly. He carried a baton topped with a carved silver rabbit's head.

'I captured this bunkin trying to break into our organization by using the old code,' said Clooney. 'He says he overheard a plot to harm the Queen.'

'The Ratzis sent him. I'm sure of it,' Belle de Paw added.

'I'd bet a pair of Jimmy Choo stilettos on it. They want my jewels!'

'Jewels stolen from the Queen and the princesses,' said Laser with a crooked grin that revealed a shining gold tooth. Belle de Paw glared at Laser who chuckled; she had more important things to do than steal jewellery.

The Generalissimo walked stiffly and slowly round the table. Shylo watched him closely. He looked wise and honest and that gave the little bunny confidence.

When the Generalissimo reached him, he put his thin face very close to Shylo's and sniffed. 'Haystacks and forests and English soil,' he said quietly. 'What's a little bunkin doing in the city, I wonder? My name is Nelson. Tell me all you know.'

Shylo felt even shyer than usual before this grand old rabbit and said nothing until Belle de Paw kicked him with one of her stilettos.

'Come on, speak up, bunkin,' said Nelson, opening his paws.

'I can only tell the rabbit with . . .' Shylo stammered and

then, suddenly, he noticed that Nelson's two front paws had red soles. 'Ah! The Rabbit with the Double Badge. *It's you!*'

'Yes, it's me,' said Nelson. 'Now get a move on. See that map there? That's how we follow all the wicked and sly plans of the Ratzis and other world enemies of the Royal Family above us. We're fighting on many fronts, bunkin. So what do you have to tell me?'

'My name is Shylo Tawny-Tail and I've come to inform you of a plot to harm the Queen,' Shylo said, summoning his courage and speaking as clearly and bravely as he could. After all he'd been through, it was as if he suddenly had no fear left in him.

'We have a lot of those, don't we?' said Nelson, and Laser folded her arms and nodded. 'Details?'

Belle de Paw laughed. 'I can't wait to hear this!' she said, rubbing her diamond-covered paws together.

Nelson lifted his chin and gave her a withering stare. 'The day we ignore a plot, Belle de Paw, is the day we endanger the security of the family we serve.'

'But of course, Generalissimo,' she gushed. 'I was just . . .' Her voice trailed off as Nelson turned his attention back to Shylo.

'Go on, little bunny. Let's hear what you have to say.'

Shylo told him what he had seen and heard in the forest. Nelson listened patiently and quietly, nodding every now and then and muttering to himself. When Shylo had finished, Nelson put his hand on the bunny's shoulder.

'Hundreds of years ago our ancestors made an oath to protect the Royal Family of England,' he told him. 'We have never failed them. We will not fail them now!'

'We will not!' repeated the entire room.

'Every man, woman, child and animal in the world, high and low, has a right to their own private heart, even in this modern world of mobile phones, internet and spaceships. When the Ratzis invade a person's privacy, they steal a fragment of their soul,' he said gravely.

Shylo's ears, which had only a moment ago flopped with

fear, now stood up straight and twitched with curiosity, for surely he had heard this speech before, from Horatio.

'Soul-Stealers,' murred Laser, narrowing her blue eyes angrily.

'You did right, little bunny, to come all the way from the countryside to find the Royal Rabbits of London. We'll foil those Ratzis!' said Nelson.

'Yes,' said Shylo, feeling very weary yet safe with the old grey rabbit. 'No one else can stop them but *you*.'

'The Royal Rabbits of London is a very secretive organization,' said Nelson. 'Most rabbits don't even believe we exist. So I'm impressed that *you*, a little bunkin, managed to find your way in. Tell me, how *did* you find us?'

'I went down a tunnel to the farm, then I hid in the farmer's van bound for London. Then I . . .'

Nelson's paw grew heavier on Shylo's shoulder. 'What I want to know is, *who* told you where to find us and *who* gave you that code?'

'Horatio said you were the only rabbits who could help,' Shylo mumbled, not sure if he should reveal how much his friend knew about this secret society.

Nelson lifted his paw as if Shylo's shoulder had scalded it. His eyes grew large. His jaw fell open and he gasped. He stepped back.

Clooney looked at Belle de Paw, who glanced at Zeno, who drew his knife. 'Say the word, Generalissimo, and I will kill him.'

'The Kennel!' hissed Belle de Paw, waving her paw in the air. 'Throw him to the Pack.'

'No, no! Leave the poor little rabbit alone,' said Nelson.

'Then, if not this bunkin, I will kill Horatio, whoever he is,' Zeno volunteered, brandishing his knife.

'Who is he?' Belle de Paw whispered.

'Yes, who *is* he?' echoed Laser, putting her paw on the handle of her whip.

'Horatio, my dear friends, is my brother,' said Nelson.

Zeno, Belle de Paw, Laser and Clooney stared back at Nelson in amazement. 'Your brother?' they said in unison.

'My brother,' he repeated, as astonished as they were. 'Horatio is *alive!*'

CHAPTER TWELVE

'Alive!' Nelson banged his fist on the map table so that the whole room vibrated. Then he threw his head back and laughed, a guffaw that sounded like gravel in a bucket.

As the tension in the room eased, Shylo felt a wave of relief. Nelson put an arm round his shoulders, embraced him and ushered him towards a sofa.

'I haven't seen Horatio since he disappeared into the Kennel thirty years ago when we were both daring young rabbits. I thought those dogs had killed him, for no rabbit has ever come out of that place alive. But Horatio survived! How on

earth did he escape, I wonder, and why did he choose to disappear?'

Shylo thought of Horatio's lost ear, the scar down his face, the bandaged paw - which he now realized must have hidden the Badge - the stump and the secret tunnel that linked his burrow to the farm and he understood that Horatio knew so much about the Royal Rabbits of London not because of his books but because he used to *be* a Royal Rabbit!

'Sit down, little bunny,' said Nelson. He summoned the four Hopster rabbits with a wave of his paw. They stood to attention, awaiting orders from the Generalissimo. 'Zeno, this is a full QOTUK alert.'

'What's QOTUK?' Shylo asked Clooney, who was standing beside him busily grooming with a small silver comb.

'Queen of the United Kingdom,' Clooney replied, bowing his ears.

'Zeno, assemble the Thumpers,' Nelson continued. 'We have a plot to foil. Belle de Paw, bring this bunkin carrots and water

101

at once. And ten sticks of celery and cream!'

CELERY! Shylo had heard that this was a great delicacy, but his poor mother could never afford any. When the celery arrived, he nibbled on it furiously and for a second forgot all about the Queen and the Ratzis. It was good, *so* good, that his head grew dizzy and he saw stars, until a firm soldier's paw gripped him on the shoulder.

'Now, little bunny . . .' said Nelson.

'Shylo,' volunteered Clooney.

'Shylo. We'll talk about Horatio when this is done, but first let's plan a strategy.' Nelson moved over to the map on the table and the model of the palace. 'Just to brief you, dear bunkin,' he said to Shylo. 'As you can see, BP is actually a square with a courtyard in the middle and gardens behind, three storeys high . . .'

'What's BP?' Shylo whispered to Clooney.

'It's short for Buckingham Palace,' Clooney replied.

Nelson continued. 'Here are the public rooms, the picture

gallery, offices, the state dining room, the guardhouse for the police, the sentry boxes for the soldiers. The headquarters of the Royal Rabbits mirror the layout of the palace above. At this moment, Shylo, we are right beneath the grandest chambers! But the family only live in a small part so all that matters to us is *this*,' and he pointed at the right-hand corner of the palace with his baton.

'The private apartments are here and the Kennels there. Now let's look at the various ways into the Queen's bedroom right *here!*' He tapped his baton on the Queen's bedroom. A trio of does started bringing reports and moving figures around in the model of the palace and on the map.

Laser borrowed a croupier stick from one of the does and pointed at the model of the palace. 'I see weak spots here, here and *here!*' she said 'We need to investigate and there's no time to lose.'

'May I formally introduce Captain Laser,' said Nelson. 'Laser is one of our best operatives, sent to us by America — she's

one of the Rabbits of the White House. Laser is hard-working, efficient and brave, though she can be a little impatient at times.'

Laser offered a paw to Shylo, who shook it. 'Pleasure to meet you, Shylo,' she said, striking a pose. 'I just like to get things done.' Then she added with a crooked grin. 'I say don't just talk the talk, you gotta walk the walk.'

'Now, Shylo,' said Nelson. 'This is how we check the palace.' He pressed a button on the edge of the table, which made the map of London disappear and a different map shine through in bright yellow lines and flashing lights. 'This shows our network of exits and entrances into every room in the palace, all the tunnels and secret doors we have built throughout the building. Genius, don't you think?'

Shylo nodded, stepping closer. 'It's amazing!' he gasped. Truly, he had never seen anything like it. What would his brothers and sisters think of him now? Standing in this secret headquarters! Talking to the Generalissimo!

Hatching secret plans!

'The trouble is, we thought we knew every exit and entrance into every room in the palace. But, if your Ratzis are telling the truth, then there is a way in that we are unaware of. And it's our business to know every bit of this place. Belle de Paw, check the royal paws.'

Belle de Paw whispered to Shylo, 'Let me show you how we watch the Royal Family. Come.' She led him to the back of the room where there was a long row of what appeared to be periscopes, lots of them, with special eyepieces to look through. Each had a label indicating the name of a room on it in big gold letters.

'Choose one,' she said to Shylo.

Shylo chose **STATE ROOM.**

Belle de Paw smiled and pulled it down: 'Good choice, little rabbit. Take a look!'

Shylo put his good eye to the periscope and gasped in wonder, for he was peering straight into a grand room — and

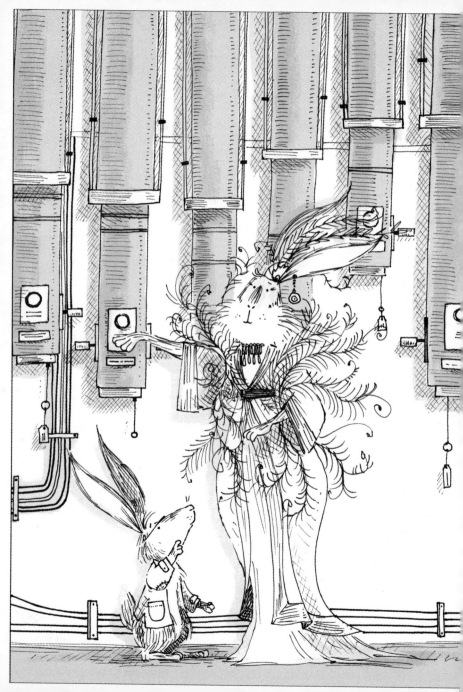

he'd never seen inside the palace before.

'But I can only make out their shoes!' he said.

'That is because we are rabbits,' she explained. 'We see the human world from this level. I recognize every shoe in the palace. Go on, tell me what you see.'

'There's a pair of plain brown shoes,' said Shylo, feeling slightly disappointed. Surely the Queen should wear jewelled slippers?

'Ladies' shoes? Sturdy, dependable, rather sensible ones?' said Belle de Paw.

'Yes, exactly those.'

'You are looking at the Queen!' she informed him, giving a little bow with her pretty ears. 'If you see shiny black brogues, they belong to the King. High-heeled stilettos with red soles belong to their daughter, the Princess of Scotland, who loves fashion and will one day be Queen. Her younger brother, the Duke of Cumbria, who rides around London on a big, noisy motorbike, wears biker boots, and his wife, who is an Indian

princess, always wears yellow-and-black Jutti shoes turned up at the toes.'

She gently nudged Shylo out of the way so she could take a look. After a moment, she reported loudly to Nelson: 'All's well at the moment, Generalissimo. The Queen is meeting a group of bakers from a biscuit factory in Lancashire.'

'Good,' said Nelson. Then he pointed at Zeno. 'Zeno, I want you and Laser to search the Queen's apartments for this secret tunnel at first light. Take Shylo too. As it was *he* who discovered the plot, it should be *he* who foils it.'

'M . . . m . . . me?' Shylo stammered, ears drooping. He hadn't thought he'd be expected to help with the actual plan. Surely these much bigger and braver Hopster rabbits should undertake such an important task?

'I'm not sure I'd be much use . . .'

'Because you're a small bunkin?' Nelson finished for him. 'Shylo, you found your way here, didn't you? I don't see the weary little rabbit who stands before me but the brave Knight

you may one day rise to be. My brother saw something in you, otherwise he would not have sent you on the dangerous journey to find us. I see it too. Courage, my dear bunkin, courage. You're braver than you know.'

Shylo pulled back his shoulders and lifted his ears. Like Horatio, Nelson believed in him and he wasn't going to let him down.

'You know what we say?' said Nelson. *'Anything in the world is possible - by will and by luck, with a moist carrot, a wet nose and a slice of mad courage!* We're counting on you. Get some rest. You'll be leaving just before dawn. Laser will show you to your room.'

'Will do,' said Laser briskly, and she winked at Shylo. 'Remember, don't just talk the talk, walk the walk.'

CHAPTER THIRTEEN

It felt like the middle of the night when Laser came to get Shylo. 'Outta bed, dopey. We gotta mission to go on!' She threw him a backpack. 'Inside are a sandwich and a cereal bar for your breakfast, and a loada cookies — the only things that will distract the Pack, and not for very long. They'd rather sink their teeth into rabbit flesh!'

Shylo gave a start, the fear once again filling his heart with dread. 'Why, if the Royal Rabbits and the dogs of the Pack are both protecting the Royal Family, are they enemies?' he asked as he climbed out of bed.

'Dogs eat rabbits — surely you know that? But there's an uglier reason, Shylo: jealousy. The Pack belong to the Queen and they don't want anyone else to get near her. They'll eat anyone who tries.'

With his heart beating wildly as he thought about those vicious dogs, Shylo followed Laser down the corridor. Zeno appeared from around the corner, chewing on the end of a carrot. He didn't look at all nervous.

'Ready, Shylo?' he asked and there was a mocking glint in his eye. 'Tell me, why the eyepatch? Did the farm cat get you?'

Shylo bristled. Zeno reached out his paw and was about to pull the elastic, as Maximilian did, when Laser grabbed his wrist and glared at him.

'Cut it out, Zeno. There's no time for that. This is an important mission and if you wanna play silly games, Shylo and I will go without you.'

Zeno chuckled. 'Shylo doesn't look fit enough to fight the Ratzis! In fact, Messalina, queen of the Pack, would probably

turn up her nose at a little scrap of fur like him.' He shrugged. 'I suppose he might do as a toothpick.'

Suddenly, Shylo's fury boiled over, for Zeno's taunting reminded him of Maximilian and his siblings. He decided then that he wasn't going to take it any more. He raised himself up as tall as he could, which wasn't even to Zeno's shoulder, and lifted his chin.

'Being small and wiry,' he said, 'may work to my advantage!'

Zeno looked surprised that a small rabbit from the countryside had answered back so boldly, but Laser smiled.

'And being clever,' she said, winking at Shylo. 'He might outwit them all.'

'We'll see,' said Zeno, throwing on his backpack. He pulled a long knife from his belt and held it in front of Shylo's face. 'You're not big enough to use one of these,' he said, handing Shylo a pair of nail scissors. 'Don't cut yourself, bunkin!'

He gave a belly laugh. 'Let's go, before the Pack wakes up. They're hungriest in the morning.'

Shylo put the scissors in his jacket pocket and hauled the backpack over his shoulders. It wasn't made for a small rabbit and he almost buckled beneath the weight. They were escorted along the narrow corridors by a squad of four Thumpers. Shylo wondered why they needed them, for Nelson had instructed them to go alone, but it soon became clear when one of the commandos opened a little wooden door at the end of the passageway.

Inside was a small wooden lift. 'This is our special way into the palace,' said Laser. 'It used to be a dumb waiter to take food up and down from the kitchen.' They climbed in and squeezed together. There was scarcely enough room for Zeno's biceps. The Marshal nodded at the Thumpers who started to pull on a rope that raised the dumb waiter up, up, up.

When they reached the top, the three rabbits rolled out and landed on an old marble counter in a deserted kitchen that had once belonged to a lady-in-waiting in the reign of Edward VII. Shylo could smell that old kitcheny smell — of chicken

grease, onions and garlic. Laser immediately leaped across to the next counter and then, very slowly and carefully, opened a two-door hatch that led into the rest of the residence.

Zeno raised a paw and mouthed, *Silence*. Shylo nodded obediently.

Laser pushed the door open a crack and peered into the room. It was dark, but for the city lights that cast a blue glow over the carpets and furniture. Laser hopped out and turned to Shylo.

'This is one of the state rooms,' she informed him in a whisper. 'There's no danger of corgis in here unless the Queen is sitting for a portrait or giving a TV interview.' She narrowed her eyes and looked about the room.

'But you can never be sure,' Zeno added. 'Those gnashing teeth are never very far away.'

If he meant to scare Shylo, it worked. The little rabbit gulped hard, dropped his backpack and watched helplessly as the cereal bar and a few cookies tumbled on to the carpet.

Zeno shook his head and clicked his tongue. 'This is ridiculous. The bungling bunkin'll get us all killed.'

'Quiet, Zeno! Come on, we don't have much time,' hissed Laser.

Shylo picked up his cereal bar and the cookies and stuffed them back in his backpack, then followed the others across the room, trying not to think of the Pack.

CHAPTER FOURTEEN

Instead of using the door, which was much too high for a rabbit to open, Laser pushed a secret panel in the skirting board, which broke away, giving them enough space to dive through and out into the corridor on the other side.

Shylo forgot all about his fear as his eyes swept over the gold-framed paintings of kings and queens. A light had been left on at the far end, which allowed him to marvel at the beautiful crimson carpets and painted ceilings. There were green velvet chairs and tall Chinese urns, and the walls were a rich crimson and gold.

Shylo was so busy looking around that he was almost left behind as Laser and Zeno marched on purposefully. He hurried to keep up as they lolloped down the long corridor. Then suddenly and without warning they froze. A pair of footmen in black trousers and scarlet tailcoats were walking up the corridor, talking to a trio of police officers.

The Hopster rabbits didn't hesitate: they knew what to do. They leaped on to one of the many shiny wooden tables that were placed against the wall. It was covered in royal knick-knacks: photographs in silver frames, enamel snuffboxes, potted plants and stuffed animals. The two rabbits hopped amid it all and struck a pose as if they, too, were stuffed and placed upon little pedestals.

Shylo had no time to think; the humans were almost upon him. He jumped on to the table and remained very still and unblinking, one hind paw in the air like a dancer, straining every nerve to hold his pose as the footmen and the police officers walked past, talking in loud voices. Then the danger

was gone and they were alone again.

'Haven't you ever seen a palace before, bunkin?' taunted Zeno, hopping lightly back on to the carpet.

'Shhhh,' hissed Laser. 'Do you wanna wake the Pack?'

They continued along the corridor until, at last, Laser stopped beside a sideboard. On top was a statue of a horse in solid silver, and beneath was a cupboard. Laser pulled open the cupboard door and disappeared inside. Zeno followed.

'Close the door behind you,' he instructed Shylo. 'And hope there isn't a corgi on the other side!' He bared his teeth and made a snarling sound before sniggering.

Shylo clenched his paws angrily, but he knew he was no match for the big Hopster rabbit. Reluctantly, he followed Zeno into the dark interior of the sideboard and closed the door behind him as he had been told. To his surprise, there was another secret panel on the other side, which allowed the rabbits to move through the wall into the Queen's private apartments.

It was dark in the Queen's sitting room. The pale dawn light dribbled in through a gap in the heavy velvet curtains. The rabbits stepped on to the carpet and looked around. Shylo's fur bristled as he scanned the room for signs of dog. He twitched his nose and sniffed the air, but it was hard to smell anything above the sweet scent of lilies and perfume, even for a rabbit with as good a nose as Shylo.

'Right,' said Laser with a very serious look on her face. 'We have to find this secret tunnel. We'll sneak into the Queen's bedroom and search every centimetre of the wall, floor and skirting board.'

'Remember,' said Zeno very fiercely, lowering his face and looking at Shylo with burning eyes. 'The Queen is here! We must respect her at all times!' They bowed with their ears.

'And what if we find the secret tunnel?' asked Shylo.

'We climb in and see where it leads and then one of us will go back and summon the Thumpers,' Laser replied.

'What if we come face to face with a Ratzi?' Shylo's stomach

had now begun to churn with nerves.

Zeno grinned. 'We fight,' he said, placing his paw on his knife. 'Or, if you're a coward, you run the other way.'

'Come on,' said Laser. 'There's no time to lose.'

They entered the Queen's bedroom by way of a secret panel, this time at the back of a bookcase. Inside, the room was dark and quiet, but Shylo sensed the presence of somebody sleeping high up in the bed that looked as big as a boat. It even had a roof on it, held up by four posts. He was so overcome with awe and respect for Her Majesty that for a moment he was unable to move.

'What's the matter, bunkin?' whispered Zeno.

'That's the Queen!' said Shylo, not quite believing he was in the same room as such an important person.

'Right,' said Zeno, and Shylo jumped at his sharp tone. 'You're never going to find the secret tunnel so you might as well make yourself useful keeping guard. Stay here and keep your ears pricked for corgis.'

Laser had already begun to run her paws over the floor and walls, moving quickly and efficiently, searching for hidden doors.

Shylo did as he was told and listened out for the enemy. At one point, the body in the bed moved and Shylo nearly jumped out of his skin. He stood, rooted to the spot like a turnip in Farmer Ploughman's field.

It didn't take long for Zeno and Laser to realize that they were getting nowhere. They beckoned Shylo over and gathered beneath the bed for an emergency meeting.

'There isn't a tunnel. I swear I've checked every bit of this room,' said Zeno.

'I agree,' said Laser. 'If there was a tunnel in here, we'd have found it by now.'

Zeno scowled at Shylo. 'Seems your Ratzi story doesn't ring true, after all!'

But Shylo was sure that the Ratzis had been speaking the truth. He put his paw to his temple and tapped the bone

there. *Where is the one place big, strong, clever Hopster rabbits might not think to look?*

Laser glanced at the light now creeping across the carpet. 'We haven't got time for this,' she said impatiently. 'The whole palace will be awake soon and we'll be trapped.'

Shylo twitched his nose. He smelled something. Something sour and farty and it was coming from the fireplace. He stiffened his ears and narrowed his eyes. Because it was springtime there was no need to light the fire, but at the back, behind the empty grate, was a large, black, lead stone. When the fire was lit, the stone got very hot and threw warmth out into the room. Shylo had seen one before, in Horatio's burrow. He scampered across the carpet and leaned into the fireplace.

'What are you doing, bunkin?' Zeno hissed. 'There's nothing in there, just a chimney that goes to the roof, or have you never seen one of those before either?'

But Laser was by his side. 'What are you thinking, Shylo?'

'No one would look in a fireplace, would they?' he said.

'Well, you're right about that. Go on.'

'It's behind that stone,' he said, pointing. 'I'm sure of it.' He climbed into the grate, not caring that his paws were sinking into the ash. His nose twitched as he now recognized the unmistakable smell of Ratzis seeping through the thin gap behind the stone. It was faint, which meant the Ratzis were still far away.

'They're coming,' said Shylo in a trembling voice. 'They're coming up a tunnel that exits right here behind this stone.' He tried to push it with his paws, but he wasn't strong enough.

'You got the brains,' said Laser with a crooked grin, stepping in behind him. 'We got the muscle. Come, Zeno. Help me shift this stone and fast, before the Ratzis do it for us.'

Annoyed that Shylo might be right, Zeno shoved him out of the way and set to work beside Laser. Suddenly, they heard the sound of dog paws: *scratchy-scratchy*. Someone was coming and they were with the Pack. The rabbits pushed and pushed, and it was a struggle even with Zeno!

He may have been a small bunny, but Shylo was determined to help. He scampered back to the others and put all his strength to the task. Together they just managed to shift the stone. Zeno scowled because there, behind it, was the secret tunnel.

Shylo gulped at the thought of jumping into the very tunnel the Ratzis were coming up, but it looked like they'd have no choice for there came a knock on the door, followed by the shiny court shoes of the Queen's lady-in-waiting, Lady Araminta Fortescue. The rabbits froze, unsure of what to do next.

'Good morning, Your Majesty,' said Lady Araminta as she opened the curtains.

'Good morning, Araminta,' said the Queen.

'Lovely morning, Your Majesty. The weather is sunny although there might be a little rain this afternoon. Nothing to worry about, only drizzle, I suspect.'

The Queen sat up, but Lady Araminta was still talking:

'Shall I draw you a bath, Your Majesty? Shirley is bringing your tea today.'

'Yes please, how lovely. Good morning, Shirley,' said the Queen, as a young maid in a white apron entered with a tray carrying a little silver pot of tea, a china teacup and saucer and a digestive biscuit on a plate. She put the tray on a table by the window.

Shylo watched in wonderment. Then, with a jolt, he was distracted by the smell of the Pack! Yes, it was the unique scent of dog - and he heard the terrifying click-clacking of little paws.

As Shirley poured the tea, the door opened wider and the Pack scampered in: yellow fur, yellow eyes, yellow teeth, short legs, a shield of white around their chests, a ruff of dark fur on their backs. Shylo, Laser and Zeno, half-hidden behind the firestone, stared at the little dogs in horror.

'Ahhh, morning, girls,' said the Queen cheerfully. 'Oh, what can you smell over there?' she exclaimed as the dogs picked

up the scent of rabbit and rushed towards the grate, teeth
bared, lips curled and snarling.

The rabbits had no choice. 'Go!' commanded Zeno,
giving Shylo a shove. The small bunny dived into the hole
and tumbled down the dark tunnel away from the dogs but
towards the Ratzis. He didn't have time to consider which
were worse.

CHAPTER FIFTEEN

Shylo landed with a thud as he crashed through a wooden trapdoor into a tunnel in a cloud of dust and dirt. Being a small, scrawny rabbit, used to taking a tumble here and there, he didn't hurt himself very much.

Laser was right behind him, but she was strong and solid and landed with a yelp (and a string of very rude words which are unprintable here). A moment later, Zeno, closing the gap in the fireplace just in time to escape the dogs, leaped after them. But in his haste he misjudged his landing and fell right on top of Laser with a dull thump and a crunch.

'I think you've broken my leg, you dumb beefcake!' Laser snarled, pushing Zeno off with a sharp shove.

'You'll be OK,' replied Zeno, looking at her leg. 'It's just badly bruised.'

'I can't move,' said Laser in frustration as she tried to stand.

'I know where we are,' said Zeno, looking around in surprise. 'We've fallen through a concealed door into one of our own tunnels. The Ratzis must have somehow found a map showing this hidden tunnel. They were almost certainly planning on climbing to the Queen's bedroom from here.'

He shook his head in disbelief. 'And we've just gone and made it easier for them! We need to call in the Thumpers before the Ratzis turn up.'

'I'm afraid there's no time to go back and get them,' said Shylo, his nose in the air. 'I can smell Ratzis!' he announced gravely. 'And they're close.'

'I don't smell Ratzis,' said Zeno. 'How can you smell them

and *I* can't?' he asked.

'My nose never lets me down,' said Shylo bashfully. 'But what shall we do? Laser can't move.'

'Never mind me,' said Laser bravely. 'Zeno, you have to get Shylo outta here. He's not a fighter. This was meant to be a mission to find the tunnel, not to fight the Ratzis.' The urgency in her voice made Shylo's heart race with panic.

'We're not leaving you here to be attacked,' said Zeno. 'We always look after our own.'

'But what about our oath?' said Laser. 'We swore we'd protect the Royal Family, whatever the cost. We can't let them get into the Queen's bedroom. It'll take too long to carry me back and you have to summon the Thumpers right away. Leave me here and I'll try and hold them back for as long as I can to give you some time.' She put her paw on her knife.

Zeno lowered his wide face, his sharp ears forward, his muscles taut. 'Laser's right, Shylo. We're all in danger, but we protect the Queen first. Corgis above, Ratzis below

and us in between.'

'But, if the Ratzis make it to the Queen's bedroom, won't the corgis get them?' Shylo asked.

'We can't be certain of that. They might have been taken back to the Kennel,' Laser replied. 'We can only rely on ourselves.'

The muscle in Zeno's jaw tightened. 'Monsters, we might not make it out of here — any of us!'

'You're gonna get outta here,' said Laser firmly, her eyes shining. 'Don't think about me! I chose a life of adventure. It was what I always wanted. I've played my part and protected those I vowed to serve with dedication and courage. I regret nothing. If it ends here, I can't say it hasn't been fun.'

Shylo wiped away a big tear, for Laser had only ever been kind to him, but there was no time for crying. 'Why don't we cut them off further down the tunnel?' he suggested, sounding a great deal braver than he felt. 'That way we won't allow them to come near Laser *or* the secret tunnel.'

'You're not going anywhere,' said Laser firmly. 'This is much too dangerous for you.' She put a paw on his arm. It reminded him of Horatio, which gave him a surge of courage. 'You've done your bit, Shylo. You should be very proud of yourself.'

But Shylo was not about to give up so easily. 'If we stand around arguing,' he said, 'the Ratzis will be upon us. Are you coming, Zeno?'

Zeno cleared his throat, irritated to be taking orders from a scrawny bunkin. 'All right, squad on point! We'll cut them off further down the tunnel,' he said, drawing his knife. 'One look at this and the Ratzis will run all the way back to their base."

'We'll come back for you, Laser, when we've seen them off,' said Shylo. He took the sandwich out of his backpack and gave it to her. 'You need this more than me,' he said.

'You're a kind bunny,' said Laser, taking it. 'Be careful. Those Ratzis have sharp teeth.'

'My wits are sharper than all their teeth,' said Shylo, pretending to be bold. If he died in this tunnel, he decided he

might as well die bravely.

Zeno and Shylo hurried off down the tunnel. The earth was damp and cold. As he hopped on, Shylo noticed the growing smell of Ratzi farts and tried to suppress a cough.

'Listen,' he said, stopping a moment to cock his ear. 'Did you hear the squeaking? They're close!'

Zeno nodded gravely and stiffened his ears.

It wasn't long before they saw torchlight glowing at the end of the stretch of tunnel and the distorted shadows of the Ratzis' fat, ugly bodies silhouetted on the wall. As the rabbits neared the corner, they heard the sound of high voices. Shylo recognized them at once as belonging to Baz, Splodge and Grimbo. They were squealing and screeching and arguing among themselves, and the stench from the rotting junk food in their rucksacks was almost overwhelming.

Zeno threw himself against the tunnel wall and slowly peered round the corner. Shylo peeked out between Zeno's legs. They saw the three greasy Ratzis looking at the screen

of a tablet. Their huge camera lenses gleamed in the dim light and their glistening pink snouts were lit up by the flickering blue screen.

'Are you sure you got it the right way round, Baz?' said Splodge.

'Of course I got it the right way round, stupid,' Baz replied, smacking Splodge on the head. 'I ain't an idiot!'

'But there are so many tunnels leading off from this one. How do we know which one takes us to the Queen's bedroom?'

'We use our nuts, dumbo!'

'What's that noise? Sounds like dogs,' said Splodge.

'Let's hurry up. If we don't get a move on, the Queen will've got dressed already,' said Grimbo.

'Don't matter; we'll just hide in her bedroom till she puts her nightie on again!' said Baz. 'You have to have patience in this business, Grimbo - didn't Papa Ratzi teach you anything?'

Suddenly, Shylo was struck with an idea that proved that he was brave, really brave. He tugged at Zeno's razor-cut fur.

'What is it, bunkin?'

'I've got an idea,' Shylo whispered. 'If I can convince the Ratzis that I'm going to show them the way to the Queen's bedroom, I might be able to lead them to the Kennel instead.'

'Are you crazy?' Zeno hissed.

'Those Ratzis will know a member of the Royal Rabbits when they see one, but shouldn't suspect *me*. I'll pretend that I live here, in this tunnel, and that, for a cut of the money, I'll show them how to get to the Queen.'

'You're going to *talk* to the Ratzis?' Zeno gasped.

'Why not?' Shylo whispered. 'We can't fight them, but I can try to outwit them!'

'*This* would work better,' said Zeno, holding up his knife.

'*One* of you against *three* of them? Even you can't beat them all on your own,' said Shylo, putting his paw gently on the blade. For the first time in his life, he really believed in himself. For the first time in his life, he really *wanted* to.

'This is the best way. But, if I do get them to the Kennel,

you *have* to be there to help me. If they get wind of what I'm going to do, they might . . .' Shylo's voice trailed off as he was filled once again with self-doubt.

'This is very dangerous,' Zeno said, 'but it's the only plan we've got. I'll carry Laser to The Grand Burrow and summon the Thumpers. You lead the Ratzis back the way we came, but, instead of going up through the fireplace, continue along the tunnel until you get to a T-junction. Take a right, then second left, and at the end of *that* tunnel you'll reach a round door that opens into a corridor in the palace. Follow that to the kitchen and at the end of the kitchen are the doors to the Kennel.

'If you can lead the Ratzis that far, I'll come back and help you. One shove and they'll all be eaten by the Pack. Let's hope the dogs don't get you first, though. Good luck, little, Monster!"

Before Shylo could reply, the Marshal of the Thumpers had disappeared into the darkness.

CHAPTER SIXTEEN

'Hey!' squealed Grimbo. 'Who's *that*?'

'Is it a little rat?' squeaked Splodge.

'I think it's a rabbit. Of all the things to meet in a tunnel in Buckingham Palace!' sniggered Baz.

'If I'm not mistaken, Splodge, he's a scrawny bunny with an eyepatch, ain't he?'

'I think you're right, Grimbo!'

'Oh bless!' said Baz.

When Shylo got closer, they stopped talking and stared at him as if he was a creature from another world. Shylo tried

to look as weak and frail as possible so they didn't suspect anything. That wasn't very hard.

'What are you doing in my tunnel?' he asked.

The rats looked from one to the other in amazement and sniggered. They knew he wasn't a Royal Rabbit of London: he was much too little.

Finally, Baz said: '*Your* tunnel?'

'Why, yes,' said Shylo. 'I live here, after all.'

'Kill 'im!' hissed Grimbo.

'Eat 'im!' snarled Splodge.

Baz held up his paw. 'I admit that I am a little peckish. It's been a while since I tasted the sweetness of rabbit pie.'

Shylo didn't have to pretend to be afraid any more: he really was petrified. In fact, he didn't think he'd ever been more terrified.

What on earth was he doing? He was trapped in a small tunnel with three large and vicious rats, who had clearly dined on rabbit before, and, although he was small and scrawny he'd

surely make a satisfying enough meal.

'However,' Baz continued, 'there ain't much to you, is there, little rabbit? I think you'll be more use to us alive than dead - for now.'

'Aw!' grumbled Grimbo. 'I bet there's more to 'im than meets the eye.'

'I was hoping for a bit of rump with a fluffy tail. That would be enough for me,' said Splodge.

'Put your claws away!' hissed Baz to the Ratzis. 'Think of the squillions of quid and our photos flashing across the world!' Then, adopting what he thought was a friendly screech, but which still sounded terrifying to Shylo, he asked: 'So you live here, do you, my dear little rabbit?'

'Yes,' said Shylo with a gulp.

'You know your way around, do you?'

'Yes,' Shylo replied.

'Then you'll know how to get to the Queen's bedroom?'

'Who doesn't?' Shylo gave what he hoped was a confident-

sounding laugh and the rats glanced at one another uneasily. 'Of course I know the way to the Queen's bedroom. But what do you want in there?'

'Never you mind,' said Baz. 'I tell you what, we'll make a deal. You get us to the Queen's bedroom and we won't eat you.'

That was met with sighs of disappointment from Splodge and Grimbo.

'Shut it, you two. If this little rabbit helps *us*, we'll help *him*, right?'

'Right, Baz,' they replied in unison.

'So walk, little rabbit, and make it speedy. If you take us the wrong way, we'll each take a limb.'

'But I want the *rump*,' complained Splodge.

'You'll get what you're given, Splodge,' said Baz. Then to Shylo: 'Walk!'

Never had Shylo been so frightened. Not on the farm, not in the van, not on any part of this adventure so far. But now

he was shaking so much that the cookies in his backpack jumped about as if they were alive. He thought of his mother, his siblings and his warm Burrow at the edge of the forest and his heart flooded with love and longing. He even missed Maximilian - his teasing was nothing compared to *this*.

The tunnel was long and dark. The Ratzis' torch shone ahead, lighting their way. Their smell was horrendous. It clung to Shylo's nostrils and made his head swim.

Eventually, they came to the place where Shylo, Laser and Zeno had fallen through the roof of the tunnel. Broken pieces of wood lay among the dirt and dust. Laser was nowhere to be seen. Shylo hoped the brave Hopster rabbit was now safely at headquarters and wished that he was there too. He hoped, he trusted, that Zeno would come back for him.

'What's this then?' Baz asked, shining his torch up the tunnel that Shylo knew went straight into the Queen's bedroom.

'That leads to the Kennel,' said Shylo quickly. 'You don't want to go up there.'

'Is that so?' said Baz, giving a shudder. 'You'd better be telling the truth or we'll rip you apart!'

'And I'll get my fluffy-tailed rump!' said Splodge, licking his lips.

Grimbo was trying to study his tablet, turning it round and round in his thin paws, struggling to work out where they were. He looked up into the tunnel above. 'But I'm sure that—'

'Come on!' Shylo interrupted. 'It's not far now. We're nearly there.'

The Ratzis followed him along the tunnel and Shylo tried to remember Zeno's instructions. *Right, second left* . . . At last, they arrived at the round door that Zeno had told him would open into the palace. Shylo put his paw on the doorknob. 'We're here.'

'We're here, we're here!' sang Splodge. 'We're going to see the Queen!'

They raised their phones and cameras ready to take a photo.

'Well, what are you waiting for?' screeched Baz.

Shylo held his breath.

'Lights!' squealed Grimbo.

'Cameras!' squeaked Splodge.

'Action!' yelled Baz.

Shylo opened the door.

CHAPTER SEVENTEEN

Shylo hopped through the door into the corridor. The three Ratzis followed, tumbling over each other in their eagerness to see the Queen.

Baz was holding his camera in his paws, ready to take the wicked photographs, while Splodge had his selfie stick poised to snap himself in the palace with the Queen. Grimbo's tongue was hanging out and he was panting with excitement, eager to send the photographs of the Queen in her nightie to the editor of *Rat-on-a-celebrity.com.*

They were staring so hard, so keenly, at their phones and

cameras that they didn't smell the Pack or pick up the patter of little paws trotting over the carpet at the other end of the corridor. But Shylo did. For a moment, he panicked. To have the Ratzis *and* the Pack so close was terrifying. But, as we've learned by now, Shylo was a clever rabbit, and he was at once struck with an idea.

'This ain't the Queen's bedroom!' bellowed Baz, looking around him. 'Where are we?' and he leaned over Shylo, drawing back his gums, and enveloped him in a stinky cloud of rat-breath.

'Come on!' Shylo beckoned, trying to remain calm. He waved his paw and set off in the opposite direction to the Pack. 'It's this way. We're nearly there.'

Knowing that the dogs were heading towards them, he pulled his backpack off his shoulder and took out the cookies. 'Ah, I'm so hungry!' he said, pretending to stuff them into his mouth, but leaving a trail of crumbs on the carpet behind him.

'If you've lied to us, we'll have your skin!' snarled Baz.

Shylo found a strength he never knew he had and raced on as quickly as his legs could carry him, scattering more crumbs behind him.

At that moment, a maid stepped into the corridor and saw the little rabbit. Her hand shot to her mouth and she let out a muffled squeak: 'A rabbit in the palace!' Then she saw the giant, ugly rats with their sloping backs and pink tails, and she let out a piercing scream before fainting.

Shylo quickened his pace, jumping over the foot of another maid who dropped her tray in fright. Its contents clattered on to the carpet, almost hitting Splodge on the head as he scurried past. Then the dogs, led by Lady Araminta Fortescue, who had left the Queen to have her bath, picked up the scent of cookie. With their noses to the ground, they sped over the carpet, lapping up the crumbs with greedy tongues.

Ahead of Shylo a pair of doors swung open and a group of servants hurried out of the kitchen to see what all the commotion was. Shylo seized the opportunity and dived

through the gap, hoping that the three fat rats were close behind him. He only had to get them across the kitchen and into the Kennel and then, with luck, the corgis would be right behind to polish them off.

Shylo jumped on to the sideboard, dodging pots and pans and chopping boards piled high with peeled parsnips and potatoes. The Ratzis were in hot pursuit; Shylo could almost feel their stinky breath on his back and he could certainly smell it, even over the aroma of freshly baked bread and sizzling bacon.

The chef, red-faced in his white hat, started to shout. He grabbed a rolling pin and began to whack the sideboard, but he missed the animals every time. Vegetables flew into the air: onions, parsnips, peppers and cabbage, carrots, potatoes and peas. It was raining delicious treats, but Shylo didn't have time to enjoy the sight because he was running for his life.

And now the corgis had picked up the scent of rabbit and rat, which was much more appealing than cookie, and were

tearing into the kitchen in a flurry of paws, tails, ears and snouts: *yelpyapyelpyapsnufflegrrrrrr* . . .

Shylo took a great leap from the sideboard and swung on the rack suspended above an island of cabinets in the middle of the room and then dived into an empty biscuit jar on the butcher's table, which rolled down the marble, on to the floor and through the double doors at the other end of the kitchen. The doors to the Kennel!

The jar shot into the Kennel, making Shylo feel dizzy as he was spun around inside it. When he felt the world stop spinning, he opened his eyes. As you might expect, the Kennel was not like any other kennel in the world. Most dog kennels are just ramshackle little wooden huts in people's gardens, but the royal corgis had a kennel that was like a giant, wooden doll's house for dogs.

Shylo gazed in wonder at the sumptuous dog baskets full of crimson velvet cushions and enormous dog bones, lined up in a row against the right-hand wall, and at the silver dog bowls

engraved with the corgis' names. Then his gaze was drawn to the dark interior of a smaller room at the back and he was sure he could make out the shadowy forms of rabbit skins on hooks, rabbit tails in bowls and dishes full of rabbit paws. The smell was worse than Tobias's rotting pigeon.

Suddenly, with high-pitched squeaks and squeals, the three furious Ratzis burst through the doors and gathered round the jar, panting heavily, claws raised. Shylo jumped in alarm.

'I'll have my rump now,' said Splodge and his sharp rat's teeth glinted like knives as he grinned.

CHAPTER EIGHTEEN

At this point, Shylo realized the horrible truth. He had lured the Ratzis to the Kennel and fulfilled his part of the plan, but where was Zeno? This was the moment the Marshal of the Thumpers was meant to rescue Shylo and he was nowhere to be seen. Where *was* he?

Then it came in a flash of clarity, like a bolt between the eyes: Zeno had betrayed him. Shylo could have kicked himself for being so utterly stupid. Why would Zeno, who hadn't even tried to hide his dislike of him from the first moment they met, come to his rescue?

Laser might have, but perhaps even she saw Shylo as a nuisance - a weak and feeble country bunny . . . Perhaps all of the Royal Rabbits wanted him out of the way, and how better than in the jaws of a Ratzi? No one would ever know the truth. And no one would be at all sorry.

His mother back home in the Warren would never know how brave Shylo had been. That, in spite of all his feebleness and his eyepatch, he had come to London, found the Royal Rabbits and talked to the vicious Ratzis to save the Queen. Even Horatio, the one rabbit who had believed in him, would never know that Shylo had discovered that there really was more to him than he'd ever imagined.

Shylo wanted to cry. But he knew that would get him nowhere. If these were his last moments, he wanted to be as brave as he could . . .

And then he smelled it: the Pack!

Baz, Splodge and Grimbo turned round to see the snarling faces of the corgis. Standing in the front, with her paws wide

and her shoulders arched, was Messalina, the biggest and most ferocious of them all. Shylo stepped slowly out of the jar and stood with his knees trembling, staring into the salivating jaws of the dogs.

'Rats and rabbits, rats and rabbits,' sang Messalina over and over again, in a soft, silky voice — and the corgis all joined in: 'Rats and rabbits, rats and rabbits,' they chanted. Grrrrrr!

'Rats *or* rabbits?' barked Lady Macbeth with a high-pitched laugh that sounded more like a hyena than a dog.

'Such a difficult decision,' yelped Lucrezia.

'Where do we start?' yapped Livia.

The Ratzis started to back away, terrified, their cameras and their phones clinking as their paws shook. Shylo backed away with them, but he knew he was in the most danger for, as scrawny as he was, he was sure he'd be easier to catch than three giant rats.

'Rats or rabbits?' the nine corgis chanted until Livia growled:

'Rats can be a little tough, but rabbit is soft and fresh. And this one looks like a tender little bunny from the country.'

'R-r-r-r-rabbit!' snarled the corgis together, fixing their sharp eyes on Shylo, and his heart leaped with panic. They bared their fangs, their eyes wild with the excitement of the chase, and Shylo realized that no amount of pleading would put them off rabbit pie.

'Let 'em eat the rabbit,' squealed Baz. 'We're going to be OK, after all.'

'When they start eating that bunny, we leg it,' suggested Grimbo.

'They can have the rabbit's rump for all I care. I'm out of here!' squeaked Splodge.

Then Shylo had another idea. Quick as a flash, he pulled out the scissors Zeno had given him. He slashed the Ratzis' rucksacks - rucksacks filled with rotting hamburgers, soggy crisps and mouldy bacon butties - and out it all poured, covering the rats.

The smell was so delicious and so rank that the corgis forgot their decision to eat rabbit first and threw themselves on to the Ratzis. As the Pack pounced, their mouths wide open for the kill, the squeals were deafening.

Shylo shut his eyes and held his breath . . .

Suddenly, a circular hole in the Kennel ceiling appeared, throwing a shaft of light into the room. Two ropes were dropped through, falling into the air like snakes. Then, sliding down them, came a pair of strapping Thumpers. Shylo was grabbed under the arms by the two rabbits and hauled off the ground.

As he dangled there, half a metre from the floor, he heard a great squeak as Splodge was set upon by the dogs. Grimbo managed to dodge out of the way, but there was nowhere to run. The dogs fell upon him too and soon his terrified squealing fell silent. The only Ratzi left was Baz. He stood in the middle of the Kennel with his paws in the air. The four dogs turned their attention to him, but they were in no hurry:

they'd play with this rat first.

Baz began to back away. 'Please, come on now,' he said. 'I'm sure we can reach some sort of agreement . . .' and the quivering in his voice and the trembling of his knees told Shylo that the leader of this small band of Ratzis was really terrified. The dogs snapped their bloodied jaws and wagged their stumpy tails, and ran after him. Shylo grimaced at the snarling and snapping of the dogs, followed by the crunching and cracking of bone. He tried to block out the noise; it was a bad sound for a rabbit — even when it was Ratzi meat between the dogs' chops.

At last, Shylo lifted his head and looked up.

Above him, holding him tightly, were the two Thumpers. One of those was Zeno.

'You didn't think I'd forgotten you, did you, bunkin?' he said with a wink and a grin. Then he added, his voice full of respect and affection: 'You're a Monster, Shylo.'

Behind the door of the royal bedchamber the Queen, now in her mauve dressing gown, had got out of bed and was sitting at the little table by the window. She was sipping her tea and eating a digestive biscuit as she had done every morning for over sixty years, and discussing the weather with Lady Araminta who now handed her the schedule for the day:

8 a.m.: breakfast

9 a.m.: meeting with the Private Secretary, Sir Marmaduke Scantum

10 a.m.: receive the clockmakers of Birmingham

10.15 a.m.: receive the Chairman of the Institute of Bee-keeping

10.30 a.m.: receive the Directors of the British Dog Federation

'What an interesting day,' said the Queen as the corgis pushed open the door with their snouts and burst into the bedroom. 'Where have you girls been?' she asked them.

'I think they've just got rather lucky, Your Majesty,' said Lady Araminta, watching them licking their chops.

'Really?' said the Queen, stroking their heads one by one. 'What did you catch?'

'Some rats in the skirting board, I suspect,' said the lady-in-waiting.

'Well, aren't you clever?' said the Queen. 'Clever, clever girls.'

CHAPTER NINETEEN

Back at The Grand Burrow, the rabbits were partying. Shylo was welcomed as a hero. The great hall was full of rabbits, and smiling faces grinned at him from every balcony. The murring of voices and thumping of hind paws rose in a great crescendo as he was escorted through the crowd.

Beside him Laser limped slightly, but she could still walk the walk, and Zeno strode tall with his chest out and his biceps bulging, but his paw rested gently on Shylo's thin shoulder. At the end of the room, on a raised platform, was Nelson. Next to him stood Clooney in his dashing tuxedo and Belle de Paw

in her ballgown.

When Shylo reached them, Nelson saluted with his baton and the Major-domo banged her staff thrice. The rabbits fell silent.

'Today is a very special day in the history of the Royal Rabbits,' said Nelson. Then he rested his kind eyes on Shylo. 'You have done something that no Outsider has ever done before. Therefore, I will do something that no leader of the Royal Rabbits has ever done before: invite a small bunkin to join our elite team of Knights.'

A thunder of thumping resounded through the hall. Shylo felt his chest expand with happiness. Never in his life had he felt so proud. He wished his mother and Horatio could see him now.

Nelson raised his paw and the hall went quiet again. 'Shylo has taught us all a lesson today. He might not be the fastest, the strongest, the most agile or even the most fearless rabbit among us, but he has shown that those things don't really

matter. What matters is the courage to be the best a rabbit can be.'

He turned to Shylo. 'So what do you say, Shylo Tawny-Tail? Will you murr the vow to protect the Royal Family from the evils of this world?'

Shylo stood as tall as he could, which wasn't very big. He lifted his chin and looked up at Laser, who was smiling down at him with a pleased expression on her face. She gave a little nod and Shylo knew that he was accepted.

He turned to Nelson. 'I will,' he murred. Once again, the hall was filled with applause. Shylo's heart swelled.

'And next . . .' rasped Nelson, nodding at an official-looking white rabbit in crimson livery who stepped forward with a tray of red paint and a medal: the Order of the Royal Rabbits of London.

Zeno took Shylo's paw and pressed it into the paint. He then held it up for everyone to see. Finally, Nelson presented Shylo with the shining medal, hanging it round his neck so

that it lay on his chest above his heart, which was so full he thought it would burst.

'Now,' shouted the Major-domo, as the cheering subsided, 'nothing makes a rabbit hungrier than adventure. The banquet is served! Let the celebration commence!'

'Well, Shylo of the Red Badge,' murred Nelson, putting his paw round him. 'Tomorrow we must find out what happened to Horatio. For now, you must enjoy the feast.'

'Will there be celery?' asked Shylo.

Nelson smiled. 'As much as you can eat.'

In a warren in deepest Northamptonshire, a mother doe was feeding her litter of noisy rabbits.

'I want more carrots!' said Maximilian, the greediest of her bunnies.

'Mother, I want more cabbage,' demanded Elvira.

'Why can't we have celery like rich rabbits in London?'

moaned Erica.

Mother Rabbit turned round, threw down her pan and ripped off her apron. 'That's it! I've had enough of you spoilt, greedy children!' she exclaimed.

She thought then of her smallest, gentlest bunny, who had been eaten by giant rats a few days before, and stifled a sob. Maximilian had told her that even he, with all his strength, had been unable to save his little brother. How she missed Shylo.

Just then there was a snuffling and rustling sound in the mouth of the Burrow above them. They all froze, eyes raised. Was it Tobias the farm cat? They barely dared breathe - until something was pushed through the hole. It rolled down the tunnel and landed with a light *plop* at Mother Rabbit's paws.

'What could this be?' she asked.

She reached down and lifted the bundle off the floor. It was a bunch of celery sticks tied with a red ribbon and there was something hanging off it. She lifted it into the light and looked

at it closely. It was a large, round medal depicting a crown with a pair of rabbit's ears sticking out of the middle - and attached to it was a label that read, simply:

From Shylo

And not far away, on the other side of the forest, a letter was delivered to the old grey rabbit, Horatio. He recognized the handwriting at once and his heart momentarily stalled. He sank into his tatty armchair and put his cracked spectacles on his nose. Slowly, with a trembling paw, he tore open the envelope and pulled out the letter, which was folded and secured with the crimson wax seal of the Royal Rabbits of London.

YOU WERE RIGHT TO SEND US SHYLO, BUT YOU WERE WRONG NOT TO COME YOURSELF.

MUCH HAS CHANGED IN THE YEARS YOU HAVE BEEN AWAY, BUT THE IMPORTANT THINGS ALWAYS STAY THE SAME: YOU'RE

MY BROTHER, HORATIO, AND A VALUABLE MEMBER OF THE ROYAL RABBITS OF LONDON. I'VE MISSED YOU. I CELEBRATE THE NEWS THAT YOU'RE ALIVE, BUT I'M CURIOUS TO KNOW HOW YOU MANAGED IT – AND WHY YOU CHOSE TO RUN AWAY.

COME SOON, BECAUSE WE HAVE A NEW MEMBER WHO HAS SHOWN TREMENDOUS COURAGE AND INTELLIGENCE. I KNOW HE'LL WANT TO TELL YOU ABOUT HIS TRIUMPH HIMSELF. LIFE IS AN ADVENTURE, BROTHER. ANYTHING IN THE WORLD IS POSSIBLE – BY WILL AND BY LUCK, WITH A MOIST CARROT, A WET NOSE AND A SLICE OF MAD COURAGE!

I AWAIT YOUR GLORIOUS RETURN.

NELSON

Horatio put his paw to his mouth and sighed. Was he ready to come out of hiding and return to his old life? Was he ready to tell his story, which wasn't only about bravery but about cowardice too? Was he ready to face Messalina and her Pack

who would have killed him in the Kennel had it not been for a lucky twist of fate?

He wasn't sure. But what kind of life was it here in the countryside, listening out for the sound of dog paws, which he believed could come at any minute, for surely the Pack would never give up searching for the only rabbit that had ever got away?

Then he thought of Shylo and a small smile crept across his face. He wasn't proud of the fact that he had hidden all these years, leaving his brother to believe him dead, but he was proud of Shylo. *Deeply* proud. Yes, he thought happily, if a weak and feeble bunkin can discover courage he never knew he had, then *he*, Horatio, could recover the courage he had lost.

He chuckled to himself. It had never crossed his mind that young Shylo Tawny-Tail would be in a position to teach him about courage.

But so it was.

Hop over the
page for some
Royal Rabbits
extras!

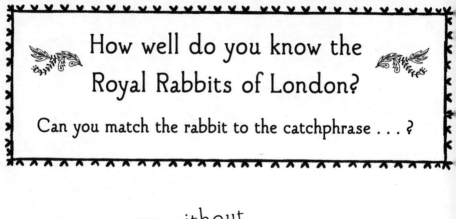
'I cannot exist without mes diamants'

'Monsters!'

'You're braver than you know'

'Don't just talk the talk, you gotta walk the walk'

'I'm sooooo handsome'

'By will and by luck, with a moist carrot, a wet nose and a slice of mad courage'

TOP TEN FACTS ABOUT BUCKINGHAM PALACE

1. Buckingham Palace is the Queen's official and main royal London home.

2. The palace has been the official London home of Britain's monarchs since 1837, when Queen Victoria moved there after her coronation.

3. Buckingham Palace was built in 1705 as the town house of the Duke of Buckingham. It used to be known as Buckingham House, but was bought by George III for his wife, Queen Charlotte. George IV began transforming it into a palace in 1826.

4. There really are secret passages running underneath Buckingham Palace, which connect the building to nearby streets.

5. The palace isn't just home to royalty - over 800 members of staff live there.

6. The palace has around 600 rooms, including 19 state rooms, 52 royal and guest bedrooms, 188 staff bedrooms, 78 bathrooms, 92 offices, a cinema and a swimming pool. It also has its own post office and police station!

7. Buckingham Palace contains 350 clocks and watches - they are wound every week by two experts who work full-time to keep them ticking!

8. When the Ballroom of Buckingham Palace first opened in 1856, it was the largest room in London.

9. There are 760 windows in the palace and they have to be cleaned every six weeks!

10. It's easy to tell if the Queen is at home. You can see her royal flag flying from the flag pole on top of Buckingham Palace. This flag is called the Royal Standard. When the Queen isn't in, the palace flies the Union Jack flag.

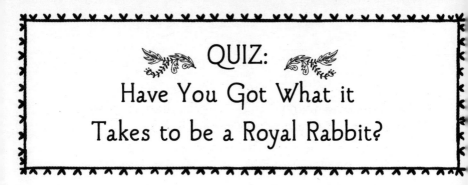

QUIZ:
Have You Got What it Takes to be a Royal Rabbit?

1. Do you like seeing embarrassing photos of celebrities?

a) Yes, of course. They're celebrities!

b) Sometimes, but only if they're really famous.

c) No, not really.

2. Walking home from school with your friend, you see a boy from school drop a £2 coin ahead of you. Do you . . . ?

a) Pick it up quickly and pop it in your pocket before anyone else sees.

b) Ignore it and carry on chatting to your friend.

c) Pick it up and chase after the boy to give it back.

3. What is your favourite way to relax?

a) Admiring your reflection in the mirror.

b) Chatting to your friends.

c) Reading a book.

4. You overhear your brother's plan to play a trick on your younger sister. Do you . . . ?

a) Not say anything. It's only a joke, after all.

b) Tell your brother he shouldn't do it, but secretly still think it's quite funny.

c) Tell her immediately and together plan another trick to get back at your brother.

5. Your friend tells you a secret about someone at school. What do you do?

a) Tell the person you sit next to in maths and then the person in front of you in the lunch queue so it's all around the school by lunchtime.

b) Tell your other friend, but only because she asked.

c) Keep it to yourself.

6. After school you see a younger girl being picked on by one of the older boys. Do you . . . ?

a) Pretend you haven't seen anything and keep walking.

b) Wait until the bully has gone and then ask the girl if she is OK and tell her to tell a teacher.

c) Go and ask the girl if she wants to walk home with you and then say you will go with her to tell a teacher.

Mostly As
You're outgoing and fun, but at the moment you don't take life seriously enough to be a Royal Rabbit.

Mostly Bs
You're trustworthy and have lots of friends, but you don't always do the right thing. Keep trying - one day you might be a new Royal Rabbit recruit!

Mostly Cs
You're loyal and brave and clever and great at keeping secrets - you're perfect Royal Rabbit material!

HOW TO SPOT A
ROYAL RABBIT

Loyal and
brave

Air of 'a rabbit
of the world'

Knowing,
important
expression

The Badge,
an unmistakable
red paint on sole
of one of the
front paws

Distinctive
clothing and a
sense of style

Q&A
WITH THE AUTHORS

1) What inspired the Royal Rabbits of
   London?

Santa: *When our son Sasha was six years old
he couldn't sleep one night. So, to help him
relax I asked him to think of something he
loved. He replied: rabbits. Then I asked him to
tell me where they lived and he said: under
Buckingham Palace. I immediately saw
the book. It was a great idea for a story. I
hurried off to tell Sebag - that's my
husband Simon's nickname - and
he too thought it was a brilliant
idea. It took us six years of plotting
and planning before we actually sat
down together to write it.*

2) What part of the story did you most enjoy writing?

Santa: *I really loved the emotional scenes. When Shylo longs to be brave and sits in the mouth of the burrow and gazes up at the stars. When he heads off down the tunnel and is very frightened and then those moments when he realises how brave he's been and feels good about himself.*

Simon: *I enjoyed writing the action scenes. When Shylo is in the tunnel and confronts the Ratzis and the chase at the end when Zeno comes good and rescues him.*

3) Do you have a favourite Royal Rabbit?

We love all the rabbits. It's too hard to choose who we like the best.

4) How did you pick the characters names?

Sebag thought of Shylo, Zeno and Belle de Paw. Our daughter Lily thought of Laser. Our son Sasha thought of Clooney. Santa thought of Horatio and Nelson.

5) What was your favourite book as a child?

Santa: *Wind in the Willows and Winnie the Pooh.*

Sebag: *Robinson Crusoe.*

6) What is your top tip for aspiring writers?

Enjoy what you write. If YOU enjoy it your readers will too.
Create a sense of place by sound, smell and sight. Your readers will feel they are there if

they can smell, hear and see the places you write about.

Don't worry about getting it perfect at the start. Get it written first then go back and polish. Just concentrate on getting the story down.

7) If you weren't a writer, what do you think you'd be doing?

Santa: I'd love to be a teacher of seven to eleven year olds.

Sebag: I'd love to be an actor.

ACKNOWLEDGEMENTS

One night seven years ago when our son Sasha was six, he couldn't sleep. 'Think of something you love,' we said. 'Rabbits,' he replied. 'Where do they live?' we asked. Sasha hesitated, then he said: 'Under Buckingham Palace.' That is how this idea was born. We soon started to imagine the magical world of the Royal Rabbits of London; the Thumpers and Ratzis, foxes and minks, from the tunnels beneath Buckingham Palace to the White House and beyond. While we were busy imagining this, we were also busy writing our other books, novels and histories. Six years passed. When we finally started the serious

yet fun enterprise of creating this world and then writing it, Sasha was thirteen and our daughter Lily, fifteen. A big thank you to Lily, who read the book as it developed and gave us very sharp and wise advice, and to Sasha for the idea - and to both of them for their love, support and mischief. We always believed in our story but we weren't sure whether anyone else would. Therefore we would like to thank those who did, and do, from the bottom of our hearts: Our wonderful agents, Sheila Crowley at Curtis Brown and Georgina Capel at Capel and Land, and Luke Speed our brilliant film agent at Curtis Brown. Ian Chapman, who stands at the helm of our publisher Simon & Schuster, and his talented and energetic team who have been key in helping us develop our idea: Jane Griffiths, Jenny Richards and Jane Tait. Of course our story would not have come to life without Kate Hindley's beautiful drawings. We are enormously grateful to Kate for her hard work and superb talent.

ABOUT THE AUTHORS

Santa Montefiore and Simon Sebag Montefiore are renowned storytellers whose globally bestselling books have been published in over forty languages. Both have written number one *Sunday Times* bestsellers. Santa Montefiore is a novelist. Simon Sebag Montefiore writes both fiction and non-fiction. They are married, have two children and live in London. This is their first book together.

Join the Royal Rabbits
on their next adventure!

SANTA
MONTEFIORE

SIMON SEBAG
MONTEFIORE

'Sweet, funny
and beautifully
illustrated'
The Times

THE
**ROYAL
RABBITS**
OF **LONDON**
ESCAPE FROM
THE TOWER

Illustrated by KATE HINDLEY